PENGUIN CLASSICS

THE TURN OF THE SCREW

SERIES ADVISOR: PHILIP HORNE

HENRY JAMES was born in 1843 in Washington Place, New York, of Scottish and Irish ancestry. His father was a prominent theologian and philosopher and his elder brother, William, also became famous as a philosopher. James attended schools in New York and later in London, Paris and Geneva, before briefly entering the Law School at Harvard in 1862. In 1865 he began to contribute reviews and short stories to American journals. He visited Europe twice as an adult before moving to Paris in 1875, where he met Flaubert, Turgenev and other literary figures. However, after a year he moved to London, where he met with such success in society that he confessed to accepting 107 invitations in the winter of 1878–9 alone. In 1898 he left London and went to live at Lamb House, Rye, Sussex. Henry James became a naturalized British citizen in 1915, and was awarded the Order of Merit in 1916, shortly before his death in February of that year.

In addition to many short stories, plays, books of criticism, biography and autobiography, and much travel writing, he wrote some twenty novels, the first of which, *Watch and Ward*, appeared serially in the *Atlantic Monthly* in 1871. His novella 'Daisy Miller' (1878) established him as a literary figure on both sides of the Atlantic. Other novels include *Roderick Hudson* (1875), *The American* (1877), *The Europeans* (1878), *Washington Square* (1880), *The Portrait of a Lady* (1881), *The Bostonians* (1886), *The Princess Casamassima* (1886), *The Tragic Muse* (1890), *The Spoils of Poynton* (1897), *What Maisie Knew* (1897), *The Awkward Age* (1899), *The Wings of the Dove* (1902), *The Ambassadors* (1903) and *The Golden Bowl* (1904).

DAVID BROMWICH is Sterling Professor of English at Yale University. His books include *Hazlitt: The Mind of a Critic* (1983) and *Skeptical Music: Essays on Modern Poetry* (2001), and he was co-editor of Henry James's *Complete Stories 1892–1898* for the Library of America.

PHILIP HORNE is a Professor of English at University College London. He is the author of *Henry James and Revision: The New York Edition* (1990); editor of *Henry James: A Life in Letters* (1999); and co-editor of *Thorold Dickinson: A World of Film* (2008). He has also edited Henry James, *A London Life & The Reverberator*; and for Penguin, Henry James, *The Tragic Muse* and *The Portrait of a Lady*, and Charles Dickens, *Oliver Twist*. He has written articles on Henry James, and on a wide range of other subjects, including telephones and literature, zombies and consumer culture, the films of Powell and Pressburger and Martin Scorsese, the texts of Emily Dickinson, and the criticism of F. R. Leavis.

HENRY JAMES

The Turn of the Screw

Edited and with an Introduction and Notes by
DAVID BROMWICH

PENGUIN BOOKS

PENGUIN CLASSICS

Published by the Penguin Group
Penguin Books Ltd, 80 Strand, London WC2R 0RL, England
Penguin Group (USA) Inc., 375 Hudson Street, New York, New York 10014, USA
Penguin Group (Canada), 90 Eglinton Avenue East, Suite 700, Toronto, Ontario, Canada M4P 2Y3 (a division of Pearson Penguin Canada Inc.)
Penguin Ireland, 25 St Stephen's Green, Dublin 2, Ireland (a division of Penguin Books Ltd)
Penguin Group (Australia), 250 Camberwell Road, Camberwell, Victoria 3124, Australia (a division of Pearson Australia Group Pty Ltd)
Penguin Books India Pvt Ltd, 11 Community Centre, Panchsheel Park, New Delhi – 110 017, India
Penguin Group (NZ), 67 Apollo Drive, Rosedale, Auckland 0632, New Zealand (a division of Pearson New Zealand Ltd)
Penguin Books (South Africa) (Pty) Ltd, 24 Sturdee Avenue, Rosebank, Johannesburg 2196, South Africa

Penguin Books Ltd, Registered Offices: 80 Strand, London WC2R 0RL, England

www.penguin.com

New York edition published 1908
Published in Penguin Classics 1986
This edition first published in Penguin Classics 2011
007

Set in Postscript Adobe Sabon
Typeset by Palimpsest Book Production Limited, Falkirk, Stirlingshire
Printed in Great Britain by Clays Ltd, St Ives plc

ISBN: 978-0-141-44135-1

www.greenpenguin.co.uk

Contents

Chronology

1843 *15 April*: HJ born at 21 Washington Place in New York City, second of five children of Henry James (1811–82), speculative theologian and social thinker, whose strict entrepreneur father had amassed wealth estimated at $3 million, one of the top ten American fortunes of his time, and his wife Mary (1810–82), daughter of James Walsh, a New York cotton merchant of Scottish origin.

1843–5 Accompanies parents to Paris and London.

1845–7 James family returns to USA and settles in Albany, New York.

1847–55 Family settles in New York City; HJ taught by tutors and in private schools.

1855–8 Family travels in Europe: Geneva, London, Paris, Boulogne-sur-Mer. Returns to USA and settles in Newport, Rhode Island.

1859–60 Family in Europe again: HJ attends scientific school, then the Academy (later the University) in Geneva. Learns German in Bonn.

September 1860: Family returns to Newport. HJ makes friends with future critic T. S. Perry (who records that HJ 'was continually writing stories, mainly of a romantic kind') and artist John La Farge.

1861–3 Injures his back helping to extinguish a fire in Newport and is exempted from military service in American Civil War (1861–5).

Autumn 1862: Enters Harvard Law School for a term. Begins to send stories to magazines.

1864 *February*: First short story, 'A Tragedy of Error', published anonymously in *Continental Monthly*.

May: Family moves to 13 Ashburton Place, Boston, Massachusetts.

October: Unsigned review published in *North American Review*.

1865 *March*: First signed tale, 'The Story of a Year', appears in *Atlantic Monthly*. HJ's criticism published in first number of the *Nation* (New York).

1866–8 Continues reviewing and writing stories.

Summer 1866: W. D. Howells, novelist, critic and influential editor, becomes a friend.

November 1866: Family moves to 20 Quincy Street, beside Harvard Yard, in Cambridge, Massachusetts.

1869 Travels for his health to England, where he meets John Ruskin, William Morris, Charles Darwin and George Eliot; also visits Switzerland and Italy.

1870 *March*: Death in USA of his much-loved cousin Minny Temple.

May: HJ, still unwell, is reluctantly back in Cambridge.

1871 *August–December*: First short novel, *Watch and Ward*, serialized in *Atlantic Monthly*.

1872–4 Accompanies invalid sister Alice and aunt Catherine Walsh ('Aunt Kate') to Europe in May. Writes travel pieces for the *Nation*. Between October 1872 and September 1874 spends periods of time in Paris, Rome, Switzerland, Homburg and Italy without his family.

Spring 1874: Begins first long novel, *Roderick Hudson*, in Florence.

September 1874: Returns to USA.

1875 *January*: Publishes *A Passionate Pilgrim, and Other Tales*, his first work to appear in book form. It is followed by *Transatlantic Sketches* (travel pieces) and then by *Roderick Hudson* in November. Spends six months in New York City (111 East 25th Street), then three in Cambridge.

11 November: Arrives at 29 rue de Luxembourg, Paris, as correspondent for the *New York Tribune*.

December: Begins new novel, *The American*.

1876 Meets Gustave Flaubert, Ivan Turgenev, Edmond de Goncourt, Alphonse Daudet, Guy de Maupassant and Émile Zola.

December: Moves to London and settles at 3 Bolton Street, just off Piccadilly.

1877 Visits Paris, Florence and Rome.

May: *The American* is published.

1878 Meets William Gladstone, Alfred Tennyson and Robert Browning.

February: Collection of essays, *French Poets and Novelists*, is the first book HJ publishes in London.

July: Novella 'Daisy Miller' serialized in *The Cornhill Magazine*; in November Harper's publish it in the USA, establishing HJ's reputation on both sides of the Atlantic.

September: Publishes novel *The Europeans*.

1879 *December*: Publishes novel *Confidence* and *Hawthorne* (critical study).

1880 *December*: Publishes novel *Washington Square*.

1881 *October*: Returns to USA; visits Cambridge.

November: Publishes novel *The Portrait of a Lady*.

1882 *January*: Death of mother. Visits New York and Washington, DC.

May: Travels back to England but returns to USA on death of father in December.

1883 *Summer*: Returns to London.

November: Fourteen-volume collected edition of fiction published by Macmillan.

December: Publishes *Portraits of Places* (travel writings).

1884 Sister Alice moves to London and settles near HJ.

September: Publishes *A Little Tour in France* (travel writings) and *Tales of Three Cities*; his important artistic statement 'The Art of Fiction' appears in *Longman's Magazine*.

Becomes a friend of R. L. Stevenson and Edmund Gosse. Writes to his American friend Grace Norton: 'I shall never marry . . . I am both happy enough and miserable enough, as it is.'

1885–6 Publishes two serial novels, *The Bostonians* and *The Princess Casamassima*.

6 March 1886: Moves into flat at 34 de Vere Gardens.

1887 *Spring and summer*: Visits Florence and Venice. Continues friendship (begun in 1880) with American novelist Constance Fenimore Woolson.

1888 Publishes novel *The Reverberator*, novella 'The Aspern Papers' and *Partial Portraits* (criticism).

1889 Collection of tales *A London Life* published.

1890 Novel *The Tragic Muse* published.

1891 Play version of *The American* has a short run in the provinces and London.

1892 *February*: Publishes *The Lesson of the Master* (story collection).

March: Death of Alice James in London.

1893 Three volumes of tales published: *The Real Thing* (March), *The Private Life* (June), *The Wheel of Time* (September).

1894 Deaths of Constance Fenimore Woolson and R. L. Stevenson.

1895 *5 January*: Play *Guy Domville* is greeted by boos and applause on its premiere at St James's Theatre; HJ abandons playwriting for many years.

Visits Ireland. Takes up cycling. Publishes two volumes of tales, *Terminations* (May) and *Embarrassments* (June).

1896 Publishes novel *The Other House*.

1897 Two novels, *The Spoils of Poynton* and *What Maisie Knew*, published.

February: Starts dictating, due to wrist problems.

September: Takes lease on Lamb House, Rye, Sussex.

1898 *June*: Moves into Lamb House. Sussex neighbours include the writers Joseph Conrad, H. G. Wells and Ford Madox Hueffer (Ford).

August: Publishes *In the Cage* (short novel).

October: 'The Turn of the Screw', ghost story included in *The Two Magics*, proves his most popular work since 'Daisy Miller'.

1899 *April*: Novel *The Awkward Age* published.

August: Buys the freehold of Lamb House.

1900 Shaves off his beard.

August: Publishes collection of tales *The Soft Side*.

Friendship with American novelist Edith Wharton develops.

1901 *February*: Publishes novel *The Sacred Fount*.
1902 *August*: Publishes novel *The Wings of the Dove*.
1903 *February*: Publishes collection of tales *The Better Sort*.
September: Publishes novel *The Ambassadors*.
October: Publishes memoir *William Wetmore Story and his Friends*.
1904 *August*: Sails to USA, his first visit for twenty-one years. Travels to New England, New York, Philadelphia, Washington, the South, St Louis, Chicago, Los Angeles and San Francisco.
November: Publishes novel *The Golden Bowl*.
1905 *January*: Is President Theodore Roosevelt's guest at the White House. Elected to the American Academy of Arts and Letters.
July: Back in Lamb House, begins revising works for the New York Edition of *The Novels and Tales of Henry James*.
October: Publishes *English Hours* (travel essays).
1906–8 Selects, arranges, writes prefaces and has illustrations made for New York Edition (published 1907–9, twenty-four volumes).
1907 *January*: Publishes *The American Scene* (travel essays).
1908 *March*: Play *The High Bid* produced at Edinburgh.
1909 *October*: Publishes *Italian Hours* (travel essays). Health problems.
1910 *August*: Travels to USA with brother William, who dies a week after their return.
October: Publishes *The Finer Grain* (tales).
1911 *August*: Returns to England.
October: Publishes *The Outcry* (novel adapted from play). Begins work on autobiography.
1912 *June*: Receives honorary doctorate from Oxford University.
October: Takes flat at 21 Carlyle Mansions, Cheyne Walk, Chelsea; suffers from shingles.
1913 *March*: Publishes *A Small Boy and Others* (first volume of autobiography). Portrait painted by John Singer Sargent for seventieth birthday.
1914 *March*: Publishes *Notes of a Son and Brother* (second volume of autobiography).
August: Outbreak of First World War; HJ becomes passion-

ately engaged with the British cause and helps Belgian refugees and wounded soldiers.

October: Publishes *Notes on Novelists.*

1915 Is made honorary president of the American Volunteer Motor Ambulance Corps.

July: Becomes a British citizen.

Writes essays about the war (collected in *Within the Rim* (1919)) and the Preface to *Letters from America* (1916) by the poet Rupert Brooke, who had died the previous year.

2 *December*: Suffers a stroke.

1916 Awarded the Order of Merit in New Year Honours.

28 *February*: Dies. After his funeral in Chelsea Old Church, his ashes are smuggled back to America by sister-in-law and buried in the family plot in Cambridge.

Philip Horne

Introduction

First-time readers should be aware that details of the plot are revealed in this Introduction.

'The Turn of the Screw' holds a unique place in the canon of Henry James's fiction. Alongside 'Daisy Miller' (1878) and *The Portrait of a Lady* (1881), it has proved the most lastingly popular of his works. Yet the prose is that of James's intricate later style, and the narration has the quality of a controlled experiment. The story turns on a question that belongs to metaphysics and morals: to what extent can our knowledge of reality be separated from the psychology of the person we rely on for a faithful description? To complicate the question, the story is offered at two removes, in the manner of historical novels like Walter Scott's or personal narratives like *Robinson Crusoe* (1719). It comes to us as a secret, long concealed but confided to a male acquaintance of the narrator's some forty years earlier; he, in turn, reads it aloud to a group of friends the night after Christmas. As for the narrator herself, she is never named and sparsely characterized, and recedes behind the words of her story. We learn that she was the youngest daughter of a country parson; that she felt a strong attachment to the man, ten years her junior, to whom she confided the manuscript; that she had been 'carried away' (13) by her immediate feeling for the master of the house that held the secret, the uncle and guardian of the children at Bly after their parents died in India. The master took the connection more coolly. He hired her to attend to their upbringing, thanked her with a press of the hand, and told her never to trouble him with any aspect of her work.

The broad outlines of the story are easily told. The boy who has been placed in her charge, Miles, turns out to have been dismissed from his school, for reasons never explained in the curt letter from the headmaster. Having experienced earlier premonitions, she sees ghosts about the house soon after the boy's return, comes to believe that the children are in danger from them, and makes it her mission to purge the place and free the children. The ghosts have identities. They are the returning form of Peter Quint, the master's valet at Bly, a man of considerable charm but brutal and unsteady habits who died a violent death in obscure circumstances; and of Miss Jessel, the previous governess, who suffered a sexual liaison with Quint and died soon after from unknown causes. The governess learns the identity of Quint after she sees a spectral figure on a tower of the house. It is the housekeeper, Mrs Grose, who judges this figure to fit exactly the description of Quint. The governess is able to supply details of his appearance she could not have known by other means. (The details and identification of Miss Jessel come later and are vaguer but are equally beyond her capacity to have learned through normal channels.) Meanwhile, the job of the governess is to take care of the children, Miles and Flora. But the sometimes unaccountable movements of the children about the house and estate, and their occasional intractability, arouse her suspicion that the ghosts are coming to exert a control over them greater than her own. This inference she soon elaborates into a theory about the moral influence of the ghosts. The governess comes to think that the purpose for which they have returned to Bly is to lure the children into hell and share its torments. Such a hypothesis runs perversely contrary to her own descriptions of the children as innocent and beautiful beings made to be loved. But the denial by both children of any awareness of non-natural presences – a denial at first tacit and later overt, by both Flora and Miles – crystallizes the fears of the governess. She instructs Mrs Grose to take Flora away from Bly, so that, alone in the house with Miles, she can wrest from him a confession of the reality of his contact with the ghost of Peter Quint. Miles says that he does not know what she means. She presses him about his expulsion from school and, concerning the cause of his discharge, Miles now gives a natural, though disturbing, account. In the story's final scene the governess is terrified to see Quint yet again, and she resolves to fight the ghost for the possession of Miles's soul. She forces Miles to confront an image which she sees and compels him to see as that of the ghost, and Miles, twisting to face her or to face the window where the shape had appeared, dies in her arms. Whether what gave the fatal shock was a confessed encounter with the ghost, or rather a sudden fear evoked by the powerful suggestion of the governess, is a point left as ambiguous as any ending of any story has ever been.

Arguments about the nature of the plot have centred on the basis of the ghosts in reality or fantasy, and the mood of possessive control or heroic virtue that holds the governess captive and prompts her to dominate others. From the necessary intricacy of such arguments, 'The Turn of the Screw' has become one of the central modern texts for understanding what interpretation *is* in literature – the grammar and limits of the perceptual process by which we sort materials for interpretation into evidence on one side and surmise on the other. An adequate exploration of the debate would take a separate essay; yet regarding certain data of the plot, no challenge has ever arisen. First, nobody except the governess can be said with assurance to have seen the ghosts. Miles and Flora deny any such contact. The housekeeper Mrs Grose has none first hand, and she fluctuates in her attitude towards the governess – surprised and impressed by the new woman's detection of Quint, but sceptical of the hyperbolic terms of love and fear the governess adopts to describe her feelings about the children. At a late moment Mrs Grose comes to think that Flora must indeed be possessed by some external force. As for the governess, before her employment at Bly she has led a sheltered life; nothing like this position has come her way before; and she is deeply anxious regarding her adequacy – swinging between extremes of delight and apprehensiveness even before the first hint of a ghost. Yet, if we suppose therefore that the ghosts are hallucinations, there remains the fact that she has never heard of Quint or Miss Jessel until her apparent glimpses of the two lead Mrs Grose to offer an account of their careers at Bly. Altogether, she sees each ghost four times: Quint on top of the tower, then lurking outside the window, then on the upstairs landing, and again pressed against the window; Miss

Jessel first at the lake, then on the stairway, then at the writing table, and again at the lake. On the last occasion, Mrs Grose stands beside the governess and affirms with perfect distinctness that she herself sees nothing.

Such are the clues. It must be added that all of the action is radically simplified. It has the melodramatic underpinnings that James favoured in earlier books such as *The American* (1877); yet here the melodramatic opportunities are not followed in the direction they point. By the conclusion nothing has been concluded about Quint and Miss Jessel. And, for a story in which a reader's attention is bound to concentrate on the plot almost exclusively, the plot has many repetitions. Its interest hangs on whether the children can be trusted in their professions to have had no contact, and whether the governess-narrator can be trusted in her assertion that Quint and Miss Jessel both haunt the house with a malevolent potency. Perception itself, as we are made to see through the exclusive emphasis on the point of view of the governess, has a persuasive power that can finally determine action; and in its demonstration of this truth about the contagiousness of a 'perspective', 'The Turn of the Screw' brings to mind such unsettling tales as Nathaniel Hawthorne's 'Young Goodman Brown' (1835) and Franz Kafka's allegory 'The Burrow' (1924). It is a peculiarly modern experiment in proving the dependency of narrative on point-of-view.

The testimony of James himself about his intentions for the story is inconsistent and elusive. It was, he says, undertaken in obedience to the conventions of the ghost story – a merely sensational genre as James considered it, meant for readers he hardly supposed to be ready for the demands of his major fiction. In a letter to H. G. Wells, he disclaimed it as 'essentially a pot-boiler and a *jeu d'esprit*'.[1] And yet he reprinted it in the New York Edition of his works in 1908, and devoted a large portion of one Preface and part of another to the artistic problems in the composition of such a tale. Here lies a second puzzle. For if 'The Turn of the Screw' is the romance of an aesthete, shaped, to the last degree, by considerations of 'atmosphere' and evoking pleasure in the sheer unfolding of its design, it is also a story of relentless torment: a device for the isolation and exhibition of human pain.

The governess is presented from the first as a character prone to touch extremes in all her judgements of people. Thus she calls Flora, on first meeting her, 'the most beautiful child I had ever seen' (12). She sleeps poorly her first night in the house because she is thinking of Flora, 'the vision of whose angelic beauty' so stirs her imaginings that it

> made me several times rise and wander about my room to take in the whole picture and prospect; to watch from my open window the faint summer dawn, to look at such stretches of the rest of the house as I could catch, and to listen, while in the fading dusk the first birds began to twitter, for the possible recurrence of a sound or two, less natural and not without but within, that I had fancied I heard. (12)

This is among the first of her premonitions. It is as if Flora's preternatural beauty generated a need for its antithesis. And in a larger sense, the children support her mental and emotional existence: 'with this joy of my children what things in the world mattered?' (30). The alternations between omens of corruption and intimations of an unearthly purity are observed acutely by Mrs Grose – in many ways a stand-in for the common sense of the reader. When, for example, a harmless comment by Miles about his capacity for mischief ('Think, you know, what I *might* do!') elicits a flutter of panic in the governess, who thinks it shows 'what he gave them a taste of at school', that judgement is judged by Mrs Grose: 'Lord, you do change!' (69). On the belief that Miles may be irredeemably 'bad', and the exalting counter-belief that he seems a being who has known nothing but love, Mrs Grose again comments: 'And if he was so bad then as that comes to, how is he such an angel now?' (53).

The governess plots and presses. Has Mrs Grose, she asks, never known Miles to be bad?

'Oh never known him – I don't pretend *that*!'

I was upset again. 'Then you *have* known him—?'

'Yes indeed, Miss, thank God!'

On reflexion I accepted this. 'You mean that a boy who never is—?'

'Is no boy for *me*!'

I held her tighter. 'You like them with the spirit to be naughty?' Then, keeping pace with her answer, 'So do I!' I eagerly brought out. 'But not to the degree to contaminate—'

'To contaminate?' – my big word left her at a loss.

I explained it. 'To corrupt.'

She stared, taking my meaning in; but it produced in her an odd laugh. 'Are you afraid he'll corrupt *you*?' (18)

This is a central passage of the story for the discernment of the narrator's motives.

Every concession and darting assumption is caught by the rhythm of the dialogue, and we are left with an unforgettable image of psychological projection – the inward fears of the governess transfigured by imagination into a palpable menace. One notices, too, the keenness of the governess to claim the largest possible moralizing weight for the Victorian nursery word *bad*. Thrown off balance by the unshockable Mrs Grose, she turns on herself with a touch of stiffness – 'You like them with the spirit to be naughty?' – and wheedles to obtain the subordinate servant's assent that such a boy might 'contaminate' others. But the terms 'contaminate' and 'corrupt' make a leap not only in the quantity but the quality of the imputed evil; Mrs Grose can only stare and wonder, and her eventual comment, 'Are you afraid he'll corrupt *you*?', has the force of an irony that traces the conscience of the governess to her fears.

The action of the final scenes of 'The Turn of the Screw' can properly be described as the extorting of a confession: 'Dear little Miles, dear little Miles, if you *knew* how I want to help you!' But the personal desire is converted into a religious duty: 'I just want you to help me to save you!' (91). So, in her mind, the governess serves at once as the advocate of Miles and his inquisitor. Even supposing he has been given 'the imagination of all evil', she says, 'all the justice within me ached for the proof that it could ever have flowered into an act' (93). Ached to find the proof or to be disabused of the suspicion? Again: 'I was ready to know the very worst that was to be known' (75). (Is this a readiness or an eager willingness?) 'He'll meet me. He'll confess. If he confesses he's saved. And if he's saved—' 'Then *you* are?' (111). (The ironic question is assigned once more to Mrs Grose.) The soul-mangling process of salvation to which the governess subjects Miles is admirable only on the theory that nothing in the world is more important than to prove that the ghosts are real.

'There was no ambiguity,' says the governess in the first scene at the lake, 'in the conviction I from one moment to another found myself forming as to what I should see straight before me and across the lake as a consequence of raising my eyes' (42). She is convinced that she will see, and then she sees. After a short pause: 'Then I again shifted my eyes – I faced what I had to face' (43). The governess confides to Mrs Grose the sureness of her vision, and of her belief that the children know what they deny any knowledge of: 'I fairly threw myself into her arms: "They *know* – it's too monstrous: they know, they know!"' (44). She is convinced that 'there are depths, depths! The more I go over it the more I see in it, and the more I see in it the more I fear. I don't know what I *don't* see, what I *don't* fear!' (45). The irony, at such a moment, requires no second person to supply. She is afraid that what she does not know will prove yet more fearful than what she does know. At the same time, she is capable of seeing anything at all, fearing anything at all.

By her second sighting of Miss Jessel at the lake, she has lost all awareness of the gap between her own and other minds: 'She's there, she's there!' (101) when Mrs Grose gives back only a 'dazed blink' (101). Her cries, again, to Flora, 'She's there, you little unhappy thing – there, there, *there*' (102), raise no answer but a child's bewilderment: 'I see nobody. I see nothing. I never *have*. I think you're cruel. I don't like you!' (103). The final sentence has the ring of authentic child-feeling that has not been tampered with; to suspect it of cunning would be to follow the governess halfway into heartlessness. In order to extract a confession, one must be proof against remorse or pity, but she is well armed for that show of strength. For to the mind of an inspired inquisitor, the very absence of evidence is the strongest proof of concealment. The sickening pathos of the story comes from the way the governess can briefly doubt herself and yet remain unregenerate: seeing the possibility that she may be wrong, she so contrives the tests that every result will confirm her theory. This applies alike to her sense of the influence of the ghosts and her sense of the rightness of her path of intervention. 'I could only get on at all,' she says, 'by taking "nature" into my confidence and my account' (so whatever she does she will think natural) – 'by treating my monstrous ordeal as a push in a direction unusual, of course, and unpleasant, but demanding after all, for a fair front, only another turn of the screw of ordinary human virtue' (114). If taking nature into her confidence acquits her at the bar of natural feeling, the 'fair front' squares her with society. She knows, however, that 'the success of my rigid will' (113) might be made to look malevolent, and so she builds up her justification with great care.

How far is the governess self-deceived? In the dialogue of Chapter XVI that marks a transition to the climax, she conveys an inference that by its omissions almost becomes a lie. Asked by Mrs Grose what the ghost of Miss Jessel has confessed to her – the truth is that no words have passed between them – she gives a picturesque answer: 'That she suffers the torments—!' (leaving her companion to fill in the blank). Yet she does not quite have the heart to call her invention the truth; and when Mrs Grose asks the direct question 'Do you mean she spoke?' the governess answers evasively: 'It came to that.' She adds of Mrs Grose's reaction to the image of the ghost enduring the penal fires of hell: 'It was this, of a truth, that made her, as she filled out my picture, gape' (86). Would the truth have made her gape as responsively as the invention did? The governess, it may be noted, here adopts the 'of an X' locution that James used often in his later fiction for purposes of sliding insinuation or a subtler-than-adjectival shading. This is one of the hints he deploys for likening the governess to an artist, and suggesting the dangers of equivocation to a mind reflecting on itself. On the other hand, the governess indulges in fabrication – no longer an economy of truth but simple falsehood – when she says that Miss Jessel 'wants Flora' in order 'to share' (86) with her the torments of the damned. The vision of that torment was a reading-in, but it interpreted an expression she saw on the face of the ghost. The detail about sharing the torments is a cheap embroidery. Yet it only projects into other worlds and on to another sufferer a martyrdom the governess early in the story has imagined for herself:

> I had an absolute certainty that I should see again what I had already seen, but something within me said that by offering myself bravely as the sole subject of such experience, by accepting, by inviting, by surmounting it all, I should serve as an expiatory victim and guard the tranquillity of the rest of the household. (38)

To risk the worst of torments is a proof of the purity of self-sacrifice.

Now as James would have known from the history of the Salem witch trials – a topic of importance for his book on Nathaniel Hawthorne, since one of Hawthorne's ancestors had been a judge at the trials – the truth of an accusation is not established by the suffering of the accuser. What, then, can we say for sure about Peter Quint and Miss Jessel? That Quint was 'much too free' with the children – and this is no small point. 'Too free with *my* boy?' asks the governess. 'Too free,' Mrs Grose replies, 'with every one' (39). The repetition suggests a want of deference, and a sexual boldness. On the reliable authority of Mrs Grose, we also learn that Quint was 'clever' and 'deep' – a contriver of alibis, and one whose actions often needed an alibi. But it is only the unreliable authority of the governess that jumps from this to a perception of Quint's fatal effect on the children. 'His effect?' asks Mrs Grose, and here the inquisitor prompts with a cringing plaintiveness: 'On innocent little precious lives' (40). The density of the adjectives is inversely proportional to the exactness of the perception.

Still, from all we are told, what the governess sees of the ghosts is real enough and is revealed to her alone. What she makes of them, however, is her creation and her responsibility. Quint and

Miss Jessel are no more the active agents of the story than are the witches in *Macbeth*. Why does she magnify them? R. P. Blackmur called 'The Turn of the Screw' the story of 'a bad conscience – a conscience vitally deprived, but vitally desperate to transform its hallucinations into reality'. The ghosts, on this critical view, are dim realities channelled to the governess's purpose to achieve effects she might have disowned with her conscious mind. The events of the plot for Blackmur issue from the exertions of 'human cruelty become conscience and motive in a personality driven, possessive, possessed'.[2] But 'cruelty become conscience' presents an extravagant paradox; Blackmur seems to have meant, rather, conscience acting as a licence for cruelty. This psychological reading brings James into the precincts of Ibsen and D. H. Lawrence – the natural historians of repression and of the deceptions by which the will refuses to know itself.

James was indeed interested in the will of the human creature to impress its power on others while denying every selfish motive. A remarkable quality of people in whom such a drive is strong is the ability to intensify credence with no addition of evidence. Their power may press outward as distortion, or inward as self-deception, but in either case it creates the imaginative equivalent of facts. Marius Bewley described *The Golden Bowl* (1904) as 'a gigantic parable in which we see how truth is fabricated out of lies'. Such a shaping of reality by personal will and design, wrote Bewley, 'ultimately degrades the dignity of the people acted on, but it invests the ones who act with a sinister interest and power'. In his essay on James in *The Complex Fate*, he went on to say that the governess was one of those persons who act rather than be acted on: she '"evokes" by a kind of sympathetic magic demons that correspond to her own hidden evil'. Thus the governess herself 'is possessed, and her possession becomes a type of the possession with which she threatens the children'. The ghosts, Bewley added, 'threaten the children only indirectly, only insofar as they act through the governess'.[3] This unsparing interpretation accounts for the earnestness with which the governess and no one else reports the sightings of both figures.

There is, it must be admitted, a teasing shadow-play about the edges of the story. James freely works both sides. When it suits him, he so sharpens the ghostly susceptibility in the mind of the narrator that she is able to carry conviction as deftly as James himself could do. The mention of Quint's 'white face of damnation' (120) convinced one of James's subtlest critics, Graham Greene, that the ghosts were a manifestation of an actual malevolence. James presses the boundary of credulity and doubt, once again, when he lets the governess speak a sentence he might easily have used elsewhere: 'I have likened it to a sentinel, but its slow wheel, for a moment, was rather the prowl of a baffled beast' (121). The beast that threatens John Marcher, the hero of 'The Beast in the Jungle' (1903), is spoken of in just that language when the voice of the narrator is James's own.

But the naturalizing explanation near the end of the story outweighs the supernatural effects. It occurs when Miles at last reveals to the governess the cause of his punishment at school. He had said, to the boys he liked, things that should not be said: 'they must have repeated them. To those *they* liked' (123). One cannot escape the conclusion that Miles spoke words for sexual feelings, sexual objects or sexual acts. And it is on hearing that 'these things' got back to the masters at the school that the governess strikes a posture flatly inquisitorial, and asks in a lunge of words: 'What *were* these things?' She speaks as 'his judge, his executioner'. Just at that moment she glimpses the hideous face of Quint against the glass, and as Miles averts himself from her severe question, 'with a single bound and an irrepressible cry' she springs 'straight upon him' (123–4). In her mind, it was Peter Quint who was the prowling beast, while she was the protector, but the image and action here suggest the opposite.

'The Turn of the Screw' first appeared in 1898, in twelve instalments in *Collier's Weekly*, before being published later that year, in separate English and American editions, as the first of two stories in *The Two Magics*. The long story that makes the second in the volume, 'Covering End', also deals with a woman taking on the management of an old house. Though the 'magic' in that instance is benign, the heroine of 'Covering End' resembles the governess of 'The Turn of the Screw' in one respect: a will-to-mastery prompts her to become the virtual proprietress of the house. This second heroine, too, though working with the comic weapons of vivacity and wit, unnerves and overwhelms all who confront her.

When James came to republish 'The Turn of the Screw' in 1908 in the New York Edition of his stories and novels, he placed it in very different company, alongside 'The Two Faces', 'The Liar' and 'The Aspern Papers'. The conjunction, this time, was not prompted by any superficial similarity of plot. It emerged from a psychological and moral affinity among the stories which James must have pondered closely. 'The Two Faces' and 'The Liar' both deal with artists – the first an arbiter of taste and fashion who plays a malicious trick on a rival by selecting unsuitable clothes for his bride at her society debut; the second, a master of portrait-painting who seeks through art to unmask a habitual liar, and by the cruelty of the process unmasks himself. 'The Aspern Papers' offers a far more disturbing parallel with 'The Turn of the Screw'. It is narrated by another unnamed protagonist, and the narration is unreliable in the sense that an ulterior meaning of the tale is suggested to the reader which escapes the perception of the teller. He is a hunter after documents – castle-combing, legacy-poaching – a 'publishing scoundrel' of the sort that believes a particular 'find' can solve the riddle of a life. The passion that drives his quest is presented as a fixed idea, like the idea of the governess that the children have a separate life hidden from her, in which they are instructed in evil by Miss Jessel and Peter Quint.

Once, near the end of 'The Aspern Papers', the narrator is exposed to his own contempt. He sees that he has counterfeited, more thoroughly than he realized, an affection for the spinster who stands to inherit the letters he wants:

> It took it out of me to think I had been so much at fault . . . I am far from remembering clearly the succession of events and feelings during this long day of confusion, which I spent entirely in wandering about . . . It only comes back to me that there were moments when I pacified my conscience and others when I lashed it into pain.

The governess has better success in pacifying her conscience; but near the climax of the action she is subject to a similar doubt – indeed the two passages offer a parallel that James must have remembered when he published the stories side by side. 'I seemed,' says the governess (after Miles has spoken of the children he likes at school),

> to float not into clearness, but into a darker obscure, and within a minute there had come to me out of my very pity the appalling alarm of his being perhaps innocent. It was for the instant confounding and bottomless, for if he *were* innocent what then on earth was I? (123)

If Miles had done nothing wrong, she would have been cheated of her mission, and when for a moment the window is clear of any face, she 'suffered', she says, 'feeling that I had nothing now there to keep him from' (123). She cannot bear to have no duty to perform. She will scare him to death rather than see her position emptied of purpose.

Not only the method of narration but the plot of 'The Turn of the Screw' depends on a premise it shares with several of James's later fictions. Something, we are made to see, must be preserved or redeemed, and it is given to one character to know the all-importance of that work; yet the character exhibits a will that crosses over from preoccupation into obsession. *The Spoils of Poynton* (1897) reveals the pattern all the more tellingly for the eccentricity of the attachment it speaks of. It is a drawing-room tragedy about succession and inheritance. Here, not human things in any usual sense but the beautiful objects in a fine house collected by a woman of taste are threatened and solicit protection. The arrayed objects of Poynton constitute the dearest part of life for Mrs Gereth; but her son Owen stands to inherit them along with the house, and he means to marry an arriviste who knows only the price of things. It becomes the duty of Mrs Gereth to transfer the objects, and with them the affections of her son, to a worthier mate. By happy accident, her young confidante Fleda Vetch falls in love with the spoils and the son; but though Owen returns her love, Fleda, being a perfect specimen of the severe conscience admired by James, cannot accept the gifts. She must prove her love to be ungrasping by a double renunciation. The two women end up together, in a smaller house called Ricks, with a few objects rearranged to mysterious effect by Mrs Gereth. Our deepest attachments, the novel says, may gravitate to things and not people, and the only charm against that seduction is to treat people as ends in themselves. Such an effort may make for unhappiness; if so, that is a price the elect in James are willing to pay. The charity of Fleda Vetch is, in this regard, a humbler version of the self-sacrifice of Milly Theale in *The Wings of the Dove* (1902).

A single detail of *The Spoils of Poynton* acquires considerable significance in the context of 'The Turn of the Screw'. Sympathy with the dead comes to be known here by contact with a ghost that haunts a scene of disappointed love. The two women speak of the discovery in an extraordinary passage near the end of the novel, where Fleda, addressing Mrs Gereth under the roof of the smaller house, attests her consciousness of 'a kind of fourth dimension' there:

> 'It's a presence, a perfume, a touch. It's a soul, a story, a life. There's ever so much more here than you and I. We're in fact just three!'
>
> 'Oh, if you count the ghosts!'
>
> 'Of course I count the ghosts. It seems to me ghosts count double – for what they were and for what they are.'

They agree there were no ghosts at Poynton because it was 'too splendidly happy', but 'henceforth there'll be a ghost or two' from the disappointed love of Fleda and Owen. Meanwhile, the ghost at Ricks, 'this dear one of ours', exerts its spell by the conveyed memory of 'a great accepted pain'. One may recall the ghost of Miss Jessel in 'The Turn of the Screw', glimpsed on the stairs, 'her body half-bowed and her head, in an attitude of woe, in her hands' (62). The same ghost is last seen 'dishonoured and tragic' and the governess denounces her, 'You terrible miserable woman!' (84). Does the ghost of Ricks with her 'great accepted pain' somehow echo Miss Jessel in a friendlier light? To see it so, one must look beyond the moralism of the governess, which represses all sympathy for the fallen woman. The catastrophe in both plots is arranged by someone of fanatical will who is prepared to sacrifice happiness and life itself on the altar of her belief in duty. Yet it is the governess, entering service in a strange house, who is burdened with the more dangerous and fragile trust. Unlike Mrs Gereth, she has children not objects to guard, and a confidante (Mrs Grose) too weak to restrain her and too deferential to offer more than a hint of admonition.

Alongside the fable of preservation and redemption, a second favourite Jamesian plot involves the penetration of a secret that borders on a crime. *The Sacred Fount* (1901) exhibits the method of relentless inquisition in the hands of a subtler person than the governess – a narrator with a refining intellect a good deal like James's own. The narrator, again unnamed, thinks he can perceive an exchange of powers vampire-like between the men and the women in two couples among the weekend guests at a country house. This ghastly fancy he mostly keeps to himself, but he enlarges its meaning from an ungovernable self-confidence, impervious to the reproaches of others. The absence of evidence counts with him, as it does for the governess, as a likely proof that evidence has been suppressed. Nor is he deterred by the thought of the improbability of his conceit: 'Nothing *is*, I admit, a miracle from the moment one's on the track of the cause.' Thus an occurrence that seems excluded by the laws of nature – that a man should grow rapidly older while his mate grows younger; that the partners of a liaison or a marriage should exchange particular traits – is rendered possible by the explanatory ingenuity of the detective. About anything that *seems* a miracle because it breaks the protocols of the laws of nature, the narrator of *The Sacred Fount* says in refutation: 'Call the thing my fact.' Can a miracle be re-described as a fact by being subsumed under my personal beliefs as 'my fact'?

This hypothesis amounts to a radical extension of pragmatism – akin to a doctrine expounded about the same time by James's brother, the psychologist and philosopher William James (1842–1910). The idea that belief not only colours but largely determines experience, including our experience of the physical world, is a familiar element of William James's essays on faith and morals.

'There are,' he wrote in 'The Will to Believe', 'cases where a fact cannot come at all unless a preliminary faith exists in its coming.' But his argument goes a long step further: '*Faith in a fact can help create the fact.*'[4] So, a ghost can hardly appear in the absence of ready faith in the mind of the person who recognizes it; nor can an artist create without an adequate faith in the rightness of his ultimate design. The narrator of *The Sacred Fount* is an artist employing his imagination on living materials. Perhaps he does so from a wrong method, perhaps with a misjudged purpose, but he is an artist none the less. As soon as one recognizes this, however, one grows uneasily aware that the same description might be applied to the governess, who speaks of her work in terms of design, craft and the proper conveyance of belief to her audience. The only difference is that she has power over her subjects. She is so placed as to produce, by acts of the will, a lasting effect on something beyond her own belief. The narrator of *The Sacred Fount* is by comparison a dabbler.

The parallel holds uncannily because the arrogance in the two cases is the same. 'I wasn't there to save *them*,' says the teller of *The Sacred Fount* of the house guests. 'I was there to save my priceless pearl of an inquiry and to harden, to that end, my heart.' The heart of the governess is hardened without her knowing it and without her suspecting she has any excess to atone for. On the contrary, she is there to save *them*. Only the texture of the narrative betrays her fondness for the pearl of her 'inquiry' and the pride that robs her of pity. There is a revelatory exchange in *The Sacred Fount* about the nature of the wonders: 'It isn't, perhaps, so much that you see them –' 'As that I perpetrate them?' The transition from the earlier to the later fable did not require a large reorientation by James. The ghosts of the first story become the postulated relationships of the second.

All of these stories – *The Spoils of Poynton*, *The Sacred Fount* and 'The Turn of the Screw' – have a peculiar after-chill. The unnatural powers retain their grip on the imagination even after a natural account of their origins has proved sufficient. But this falls in with a pattern of romance psychology by which a mystery may outlast its exposure: E. T. A. Hoffmann's short story 'The Sandman' (1816) and Alfred Hitchcock's film *Vertigo* (1958) are conspicuous examples. In a story like 'The Turn of the Screw', we are made to see the conquest of probability as the reward of a wilful imagination. (If the story were told in the third person, the disproportion between the will of the governess and the weaker wills of the other characters would be even more marked.) But she clutches the reader, too. She holds us so in her grip that we feel – against probability, against a plain demonstrated truth of psychology – that she may truly have discerned the malignity of an external influence. The idea persists beyond all we know of the way she has produced the effects that she describes.

The magical moments hardest to naturalize are Miles's standing alone outside in the dark as he gazes up at the house where Quint is supposed to beckon; and later, the dreadful curses that come out of Flora, as reported by Mrs Grose, which seem traceable to no earthly source. By contrast, the last scene with Miles is finely balanced to tip the reader in whatever direction the reader's belief was already tending. The question whether Miles sees Quint or only sees the governess horribly grimace and scream – this becomes a matter to be settled by the reader's inclination. Yet her passion, her isolation, and her prominence in the story work to favour the claims of the governess. Lack of imagination would have left things at Bly as they were; perhaps the life of Miles would have been spared; yet we naturally side with action over inertia. Besides, the story affords no counter-voice to remind us that there may have been no corruption to remedy. The imagination, however, has its own fanaticism, and its own cruelty. The disturbance many readers have felt at the end of 'The Turn of the Screw' comes from a stand-off between imagination, which creates the objects it works upon and works against, and an instinct of delicacy or prudence or mere decency that forbears to tamper with bodies and souls even in the cause of purification.

None of the stories that invites comparison with 'The Turn of the Screw', and none of the stories James ever printed alongside it, is a ghost story. Rather they are stories about will and belief. Still, James did write several stories about ghosts, and it seems likely that he believed in ghosts. Believed as a matter of experience and not metaphysical truth; a kind of experience which he did not profess to have had, but which was interesting in fiction for the light it could throw on the experiencer. In all these elements of his imaginative stance, Henry James was at one with his brother. Well-attested experiences of ghosts, wrote William James in 'What Psychical Research Has Accomplished' (1897), are 'but extreme manifestations of a common truth – the truth that the invisible segments of our minds are susceptible, under rarely realized conditions, of acting and being acted upon by the invisible segments of other conscious lives'. William James, in short, declined to accept the terms of the rational dilemma whereby an apparently non-natural force must either be what it claims to be, or be classified at once as sheer imposture. A characteristic of genuine science is that it 'always takes a known kind of phenomenon, and tries to extend its range'.[5] As, therefore, concerning our own minds we know that we cannot be fully aware of the instincts, motives and stored perceptions that constitute it, yet we grant that such hidden elements are present, so with entities like ghosts which have some of the properties of minds, we can understand their significance best by studying them in conjunction with ourselves.

A vulgar curiosity regarding the *precise boundary* between material and immaterial existence may prevent our recognizing how much the two have in common. For 'the only complete category of our thinking', according to William James, 'is the category of personality', and personality itself, rightly regarded, is 'a condition of events'.[6] It is this that unites what we know of the material and immaterial realms. Henry James agreed and said so in many places, most memorably in his essay on Ivan Turgenev (1874) and in the Preface to the New York Edition of *The Portrait of a Lady* (1908). To accept that truth about personality entails an extension as well as a limitation of our interest in the supernatural. It follows for example, as William James noted, that 'upheavals from the subliminal into the supraliminal region', such as hallucinations and sudden impulses, may depend on the access afforded by a given personality to stimuli from an unknown source. And ghosts (as much as human reports of ghosts) may lie. In 'The Final Impressions of a Psychical Researcher' (1909), William James concluded: 'Our subconscious region seems, as a rule, to be dominated either by a crazy "will to make-believe," or by some curious external force impelling us to personation.'[7] This holds true for the way mediums may take on experiences to which their lives afford no clue – experiences drawn from what William James called 'outer space'. It holds equally for the dead entering the minds of the living, persons achieving a more-than-natural sympathy with others, and the living attaining a matter-of-fact companionship with the dead, as happens in Henry James's story 'The Way It Came' (1896). The difference, William James observed without fanfare, between philosophical scholars of psychical research and ordinary people is merely that the latter, while acknowledging the existence of unaccountable phenomena, suppose them to be quite rare whereas the former know them to be common.

Thus, on William James's view, there could be no accurate explanation of the ghosts seen by the governess without an understanding of the personality of the governess. For such revelations work through incorrigibly human mediums, and they work only on susceptible minds. Certain phenomena or creatures or survivals of earthly experience may penetrate a 'gifted' consciousness even as they are rejected by the consciousness whose barriers remain higher. Yet what the medium hears or the perceiver reconstructs is never separable from the personality, the accessibility to experience, and the ordinary knowledge of the bearer of the extraordinary awareness. The report of a ghost tells us something about the reporter. If, then, we say the ghosts are real in 'The Turn of the Screw', we must add that their reality is conditioned by the character and the situation of the governess.

An apparent perplexity about the story may be seen to have vanished once we acknowledge that the governess is the main actor and the demons evidently do not act themselves. We may accept that Quint and Miss Jessel exist while affirming it is the governess who produces effects. The germ of the story, in an anecdote conveyed to James by the Archbishop of Canterbury, had allowed for no such complexity. As James recorded it in his notebook:

> The servants, wicked and depraved, corrupt and deprave the children; the children are bad, full of evil, to a sinister degree. The servants *die* (the story vague about the way of it) and their apparitions, figures, return to haunt the house *and* children, to whom they seem to beckon, whom they invite and solicit, from across dangerous places, the deep ditch of a sunk fence, etc. – so that the children may destroy themselves, lose themselves, by responding, by getting into their power.[8]

Cues from the notebook entry survive in the scenes of beckoning from the tower and the lake, and the search for a quarry by the dreadful visage of Quint at the windowpane. Yet the idea familiar from *Hamlet* that a ghost may incite self-destruction – 'What if it tempt you toward the flood, my lord?' – scarcely enters the final texture of the story.

James gave a better clue to the effects he did and did not desire in his Preface to the volume of the New York Edition that included 'The Altar of the Dead', 'The Real Right Thing' and 'Sir Edmund Orme'. Of the artistic rendering of a supernatural phenomenon, he remarked that 'we want it clear, goodness knows, but we also want it thick, and we get the thickness in the human consciousness that entertains and records, that amplifies and interprets it.' Prodigies coming 'straight' produced for him an inferior sensation. 'They keep all their character, on the other hand, by looming through some other history – the indispensable history of somebody's *normal* relation to something.' He means by history just what William James meant by personality – a clue that the heart of the interest, for him, could only have been the governess. In the Preface to the volume that contains 'The Turn of the Screw' along with 'The Aspern Papers', the relevant section of which is reprinted in this Penguin Classics edition, James followed the same clue and said of Quint and Miss Jessel that they were 'not "ghosts" at all . . . but goblins, elves, imps, demons as loosely constructed as those of the old trials for witchcraft' (130). This way of putting it does not vouch for the reality of 'goblins, elves, imps' so much as it uses the testimony about them to illustrate the character of those who witness such prodigies. When James says that his ghosts are 'loosely constructed', he means that they are not built to withstand rational scrutiny: a fact about their composition that the governess does not realize. 'The essence of the matter,' he declared in the same Preface, 'was the villainy of motive in the evoked predatory creatures' (130), but the apparent revelation here is teasingly elusive. *Evoked*, of course, is the critical word, but the motive in question is not necessarily that of the demons alone. James does not say who or what causes the action. What is clear is that he, as author, has evoked a motive in the demons, just as the governess has evoked a response in the children.

Writing to friends about the story, he inched towards an acknowledgement of the centrality of the governess. It was modest but not quite ingenuous of him to have told H. G. Wells 'The Turn of the Screw' was a pot-boiler. To F. W. H. Myers (a leader in the field of psychical research), he wrote more assertively that his interest was 'the communication to the children of the most infernal imaginable evil and danger'; what ought to engage the reader is therefore the 'condition, on their part, of being as *exposed* as we can humanly conceive children to be'.[9] But exposed to what? The evil that threatens them is channelled and communicated by the governess.

'It remains for the future to decide,' wrote Sigmund Freud in his interpretation of the Schreber case, 'whether there is more delusion in my theory than I should like to admit, or whether there is more truth in Schreber's delusion than other people are as yet prepared to believe.'[10] James took an absorbing interest in the same perplexity. What authority can we give to the wild interpretation of a wild phenomenon? One comes back to the deepest of mysteries of the imagination, namely the power a delusion may possess to outlast its sensible refutation. The final paragraphs of the story are so disturbing because we see there the destruction of a life; yet we witness the death of Miles as an event whose cause can never be traced and a crime that cannot be punished. There is an aftertaste, as well, that had better be acknowledged by an admirer of Henry James. Masterly though the story is, its texture is marked by an almost predatory craving for order and symmetry. The phrase 'the turn of the screw' refers to the claim by the governess that in her forcing of Miles, she was only performing 'another turn of the screw of ordinary human virtue', but the same phrase had been used earlier in a context that linked it more nearly to James than to this narrator. 'If,' says Douglas, the frame-story narrator to whom the manuscript has been confided – if 'the child' in a ghost story 'gives the effect of another turn of the screw, what do you say to *two* children—?' (3). It is a perverse upping of the ante, and refers to a connoisseurship of cruelty. The same detachment carries into the comment by James in his Preface that 'my values are positively all blanks save so far as an excited horror, a promoted pity, a created expertness – on which punctual effects of strong causes no writer can ever fail to plume himself – proceed to read into them more or less fantastic figures' (131–2). He commends the tale for a skilful use of 'blanks' that directs a reader's attention to nothing but the writer's accomplished design.

James took this kind of story further than Wilkie Collins or Robert Louis Stevenson had done. He made its essence psychological even as he retained the surface proprieties of a sensational action. Bafflement at the contradiction – a confusion that, as we have seen, is kept up in James's own letters – explains some part of the contemporary reaction to the story. Yet the stunned and reproachful language of certain early reviews suggests a response more sensitive than the complacent endorsements of academic interpreters. 'The feeling after perusal of the horrible story,' wrote a reviewer for *The Independent* of Long Island on 5 January 1899, 'is that one has been assisting in an outrage upon the holiest and sweetest fountain of human innocence, and helping to debauch – at least by helplessly standing by – the pure and trusting nature of children.'[11] The prudery here is only apparent, for the writer has got a whiff of a betrayal embedded in the story, a remedy that scalds where it promised to soothe. The governess seems to be trustworthy, and her relentless grip of her duty seems to point to a happy ending. Yet we are never sufficiently persuaded of her sanity to accept that she saves Miles from a damnation that exists outside her mind. And the same review brings out another troubling fact. Though the ghosts are unholy, there can be nothing debauched about the progress of the tale unless we suppose the governess to be a sinister force. The reviewer has sensed this without being able to put it into words. The unpleasant truth is admitted at the start – in some measure to inoculate us against the outrage – by the frame-narrator Douglas: he knows nothing to equal this tale, he says, 'for dreadful – dreadfulness!' or 'for general uncanny ugliness and horror and pain' (4). The horror and pain are certainly exorbitant if we see the children as tortured by a conflict into which the governess draws them unwilling.

Were this the narrative of a girl being sent away from a haunted house, and her brother staying and dying of fright, it would not support such a weight of disturbed appreciation. But, after all, the deepest charge of horror and pain is detonated by the governess – by her credibility and her monstrous will alike, and the seductive insistence with which she acts as an intermediary with the ghosts. It is this that sharpens the torment for the reader as it did for the children. The difference is that the children have to regard her as mad (in which case their lives are in the hands of a lunatic) or else as possessed by the vision of a terrible truth. Whereas the reader is free to judge the mind of the governess by its exhibited inversions and projections and its apparent unintended effects. In 'The Turn of the Screw', we are shown the most dangerous imaginable case of a confusion between the duties of conscience and the emergence of a fantastic self-will out of the soil of suppressed passion. The narrative of the governess discloses the power of fiction to create reality by conjuring actual effects from inward beliefs. We who read are spared the effects by being allowed to witness the process. We are given the materials for an explanation of the way the beliefs were formed. We come to know in response to what secreted terrors the demons took on their final ominous shape. Yet to recognize the human source of a more than human terror renders our pity and self-doubt not a shade less unsettling and not a layer less inscrutable.

NOTES

See Further Reading for full publishing details if not given below.

1. Letter to H. G. Wells, 9 December 1898, in *Henry James: Letters*, ed. Leon Edel, vol. IV, p. 86.
2. R. P. Blackmur, *Studies in Henry James*, ed. Veronica A. Makowsky, pp. 168, 169.
3. Marius Bewley, *The Complex Fate*, pp. 87, 91, 110.
4. William James, *The Will to Believe and Other Essays in Popular Philosophy* (New York: Longman, Green and Co., 1907), p. 25.
5. William James, 'What Psychical Research Has Accomplished', in *William James on Psychical Research*, ed. Gardner Murphy and Robert O. Ballou (New York: Viking Press, 1960), p. 42.
6. Ibid., p. 47.
7. 'The Final Impressions of a Psychical Researcher', in *William James on Psychical Research*, p. 322.
8. Henry James, *Complete Notebooks*, ed. Leon Edel and Lyall H. Powers, p. 109.
9. Letter to F. W. H. Myers, 19 December 1898, in *Henry James: Letters*, vol. IV, p. 88.
10. Sigmund Freud, 'Psycho-Analytic Notes on an Autobiographical Account of a Case of Paranoia', in *Complete Psychological Works*, 24 vols. (London: Hogarth Press, 1955–74), vol. 12, p. 79. Freud diagnosed the psychosis of Daniel Paul Schreber, who believed that God was turning him into a woman, as an emanation of Schreber's wish to submit himself to his father. The sentence is quoted by Shoshana Felman in 'Turning the Screw of Interpretation', which traces a repetitive pattern of blindness and demystification that James's story is said to pass from the governess to every interpreter.
11. *The Turn of the Screw*, Norton Critical Edition, ed. Deborah Esch and Jonathan Warren, second edn. (New York: W. W. Norton & Co., 1999), p. 156.

Further Reading

BY HENRY JAMES

Autobiography, ed. Frederick W. Dupee (New York: Criterion Books, 1956).

The Complete Letters of Henry James, ed. Pierre A. Walker and Greg Zacharias (Lincoln, NE: University of Nebraska, 2006–).

The Complete Notebooks of Henry James, ed. Leon Edel and Lyall H. Powers (New York and Oxford: Oxford University Press, 1987).

The Complete Plays of Henry James, ed. Leon Edel (London: Rupert Hart-Davis, 1949).

Complete Stories, 5 vols. (New York and Cambridge: Library of America, 1996–9).

Henry James: Letters, ed. Leon Edel, 4 vols. (Cambridge, MA, and London: Belknap Press, 1974–84).

The Letters of Henry James, ed. Percy Lubbock, 2 vols. (London: Macmillan, 1920).

Literary Criticism, ed. Leon Edel and Mark Wilson, 2 vols. (New York: Library of America, 1984).

New York Edition of *The Novels and Tales of Henry James*, 24 vols. (New York/London: Scribner/Macmillan, 1907–9).

BIOGRAPHY, CRITICISM AND REFERENCE

Blackmur, R. P., *Studies in Henry James*, ed. Veronica A. Makowsky (New York: New Directions, 1983).

Chase, Richard, *The American Novel and its Tradition* (Garden City, NY: Doubleday, 1957).
Dupee, F .W., *Henry James: His Life and Writings* (New York: William Sloane, 1951).
Edel, Leon, *Henry James*, 5 vols. (New York: Lippincott, 1953–1972).
Holland, Laurence Bedwell, *The Expense of Vision: Essays on the Craft of Henry James* (Princeton: Princeton University Press, 1964).
Horne, Philip (ed.), *Henry James: A Life in Letters* (London: Penguin, 1999).
——, *Henry James and Revision: The New York Edition* (Oxford: Oxford University Press, 1990).
Kaplan, Fred, *Henry James: The Imagination of Genius* (London: Hodder & Stoughton, 1992).
Lewis, R. W. B., *The Jameses: A Family Narrative* (New York: Farrar, Straus and Giroux, 1991).
Matthiessen, F. O., *Henry James: The Major Phase* (New York: Oxford University Press, 1944).
Novick, Sheldon M., *Henry James*, 2 vols. (New York: Random House, 1996–2007).
Pippin, Robert B., *Henry James and the Modern Moral Life* (Cambridge: Cambridge University Press, 2000).
Posnock, Ross, *The Trial of Curiosity* (Oxford: Oxford University Press, 1991).
Wilson, Edmund, *The Triple Thinkers* (New York: Oxford University Press, 1948).
Yeazell, Ruth, *Language and Knowledge in the Late Novels of Henry James* (Chicago: University of Chicago Press, 1976).

CRITICAL WORKS RELATING TO 'THE TURN OF THE SCREW'

Beidler, Peter G., *Ghosts, Demons, and Henry James* (Columbia, MO: University of Missouri Press, 1989).
Bewley, Marius, *The Complex Fate* (London: Chatto & Windus, 1952).

Felman, Shoshana, 'Turning the Screw of Interpretation', *Yale French Studies*, 55/56 (1977), pp. 94–207.

Hadley, Tessa, *Henry James and the Imagination of Pleasure* (Cambridge: Cambridge University Press, 2002).

Heller, Terry, *The Turn of the Screw: Bewildered Vision* (Boston: Twayne, 1989).

Goddard, Harold C., 'A Pre-Freudian Reading of *The Turn of the Screw*', *Nineteenth Century Literature*, 12 (1957), pp. 1–36.

Kenton, Edna, 'Henry James to the Ruminant Reader: The Turn of the Screw', *The Arts*, VI (1924), pp. 245–55.

Lustig, T. J., *Henry James and the Ghostly* (Cambridge: Cambridge University Press, 1994).

Pollack, Vivian R. (ed.), *New Essays on Daisy Miller and The Turn of the Screw* (Cambridge: Cambridge University Press, 1993).

A Note on the Text

The present edition follows the text of volume 12 of the New York Edition of *The Novels and Tales of Henry James*, published in 1908. It incorporates James's final revisions, and is, in the judgement of the present editor, the most finished and satisfying version of the story.

The following characteristics of the New York Edition have been brought into conformity with modern British practice: double quotation marks are set as single; m-rule dashes that occur in mid-sentence become spaced n-rule dashes; 'ise' endings are replaced by 'ize'; contractions opened by James (e.g. 'have n't') are closed up ('haven't'); and close-quotation marks for a single word or phrase in inverted commas are placed before rather than after a comma (e.g. '"The Turn of the Screw",' instead of '"The Turn of the Screw,"').

THE TURN OF THE SCREW

The story had held us, round the fire, sufficiently breathless, but except the obvious remark that it was gruesome, as on Christmas Eve in an old house a strange tale should essentially be, I remember no comment uttered till somebody happened to note it as the only case he had met in which such a visitation had fallen on a child. The case, I may mention, was that of an apparition in just such an old house as had gathered us for the occasion – an appearance, of a dreadful kind, to a little boy sleeping in the room with his mother and waking her up in the terror of it; waking her not to dissipate his dread and soothe him to sleep again, but to encounter also herself, before she had succeeded in doing so, the same sight that had shocked him. It was this observation that drew from Douglas – not immediately, but later in the evening – a reply that had the interesting consequence to which I call attention. Someone else told a story not particularly effective, which I saw he was not following. This I took for a sign that he had himself something to produce and that we should only have to wait. We waited in fact till two nights later; but that same evening, before we scattered, he brought out what was in his mind.

'I quite agree – in regard to Griffin's ghost, or whatever it was – that its appearing first to the little boy, at so tender an age, adds a particular touch. But it's not the first occurrence of its charming kind that I know to have been concerned with a child. If the child gives the effect another turn of the screw, what do you say to *two* children—?'

'We say of course,' somebody exclaimed, 'that two children give two turns! Also that we want to hear about them.'

I can see Douglas there before the fire, to which he had got up to present his back, looking down at this converser with his hands in his pockets. 'Nobody but me, till now, has ever heard. It's quite too horrible.' This was naturally declared by several voices to give the thing the utmost price, and our friend, with quiet art, prepared his triumph by turning his eyes over the rest of us and going on: 'It's beyond everything. Nothing at all that I know touches it.'

'For sheer terror?' I remember asking.

He seemed to say it wasn't so simple as that; to be really at a loss how to qualify it. He passed his hand over his eyes, made a little wincing grimace. 'For dreadful – dreadfulness!'

'Oh how delicious!' cried one of the women.

He took no notice of her; he looked at me, but as if, instead of me, he saw what he spoke of. 'For general uncanny ugliness and horror and pain.'

'Well then,' I said, 'just sit right down and begin.'

He turned round to the fire, gave a kick to a log, watched it an instant. Then as he faced us again: 'I can't begin. I shall have to send to town.' There was a unanimous groan at this, and much reproach; after which, in his preoccupied way, he explained. 'The story's written. It's in a locked drawer – it has not been out for years. I could write to my man and enclose the key; he could send down the packet as he finds it.' It was to me in particular that he appeared to propound this – appeared almost to appeal for aid not to hesitate. He had broken a thickness of ice, the formation of many a winter; had had his reasons for a long silence. The others resented postponement, but it was just his scruples that charmed me. I adjured him to write by the first post and to agree with us for an early hearing; then I asked him if the experience in question had been his own. To this his answer was prompt. 'Oh thank God, no!'

'And is the record yours? You took the thing down?'

'Nothing but the impression. I took that *here*' – he tapped his heart. 'I've never lost it.'

'Then your manuscript—?'

'Is in old faded ink and in the most beautiful hand.' He hung fire again. 'A woman's. She has been dead these twenty years.

She sent me the pages in question before she died.' They were all listening now, and of course there was somebody to be arch, or at any rate to draw the inference. But if he put the inference by without a smile it was also without irritation. 'She was a most charming person, but she was ten years older than I. She was my sister's governess,' he quietly said. 'She was the most agreeable woman I've ever known in her position; she'd have been worthy of any whatever. It was long ago, and this episode was long before. I was at Trinity, and I found her at home on my coming down the second summer. I was much there that year – it was a beautiful one; and we had, in her off-hours, some strolls and talks in the garden – talks in which she struck me as awfully clever and nice. Oh yes; don't grin: I liked her extremely and am glad to this day to think she liked me too. If she hadn't she wouldn't have told me. She had never told any one. It wasn't simply that she said so, but that I knew she hadn't. I was sure; I could see. You'll easily judge why when you hear.'

'Because the thing had been such a scare?'

He continued to fix me. 'You'll easily judge,' he repeated: '*you* will.'

I fixed him too. 'I see. She was in love.'

He laughed for the first time. 'You *are* acute. Yes, she was in love. That is she *had* been. That came out – she couldn't tell her story without its coming out. I saw it, and she saw I saw it; but neither of us spoke of it. I remember the time and the place – the corner of the lawn, the shade of the great beeches and the long hot summer afternoon. It wasn't a scene for a shudder; but oh—!' He quitted the fire and dropped back into his chair.

'You'll receive the packet Thursday morning?' I said.

'Probably not till the second post.'

'Well then; after dinner—'

'You'll all meet me here?' He looked us round again. 'Isn't anybody going?' It was almost the tone of hope.

'Everybody will stay!'

'*I* will – and *I* will!' cried the ladies whose departure had been fixed. Mrs. Griffin, however, expressed the need for a little more light. 'Who was it she was in love with?'

'The story will tell,' I took upon myself to reply.

'Oh I can't wait for the story!'

'The story *won't* tell,' said Douglas; 'not in any literal vulgar way.'

'More's the pity then. That's the only way I ever understand.'

'Won't *you* tell, Douglas?' somebody else enquired.

He sprang to his feet again. 'Yes – to-morrow. Now I must go to bed. Good-night.' And, quickly catching up a candlestick, he left us slightly bewildered. From our end of the great brown hall we heard his step on the stair; whereupon Mrs. Griffin spoke. 'Well, if I don't know who she was in love with I know who *he* was.'

'She was ten years older,' said her husband.

'*Raison de plus*[1] – at that age! But it's rather nice, his long reticence.'

'Forty years!' Griffin put in.

'With this outbreak at last.'

'The outbreak,' I returned, 'will make a tremendous occasion of Thursday night'; and every one so agreed with me that in the light of it we lost all attention for everything else. The last story, however incomplete and like the mere opening of a serial, had been told; we handshook and 'candlestuck', as somebody said, and went to bed.

I knew the next day that a letter containing the key had, by the first post, gone off to his London apartments; but in spite of – or perhaps just on account of – the eventual diffusion of this knowledge we quite let him alone till after dinner, till such an hour of the evening in fact as might best accord with the kind of emotion on which our hopes were fixed. Then he became as communicative as we could desire, and indeed gave us his best reason for being so. We had it from him again before the fire in the hall, as we had had our mild wonders of the previous night. It appeared that the narrative he had promised to read us really required for a proper intelligence a few words of prologue. Let me say here distinctly, to have done with it, that this narrative, from an exact transcript of my own made much later, is what I shall presently give. Poor Douglas, before his death – when it was in sight – committed to me the manuscript that reached him on the third of these days and that, on the same spot, with immense effect, he began to read to our hushed little circle on the night of the fourth. The departing ladies who had said they would stay didn't, of course, thank heaven, stay: they departed, in consequence of arrangements made, in a rage of curiosity, as they professed, produced by the touches with which he had already worked us up. But that only made his little final auditory more compact and select, kept it, round the hearth, subject to a common thrill.

The first of these touches conveyed that the written statement took up the tale at a point after it had, in a manner, begun. The fact to be in possession of was therefore that his old friend, the youngest of several daughters of a poor country parson, had at the age of twenty, on taking service for the first time in the schoolroom, come up to London, in trepidation, to answer in person an advertisement that had already placed her in brief correspondence with the advertiser. This person proved, on her presenting herself for judgement at a house in Harley Street[2] that impressed her as vast and imposing – this prospective patron proved a gentleman, a bachelor in the prime of life, such a figure as had never risen, save in a dream or an old novel, before a fluttered anxious girl out of a Hampshire vicarage. One could easily fix his type; it never, happily, dies out. He was handsome and bold and pleasant, off-hand and gay and kind. He struck her, inevitably, as gallant and splendid, but what took her most of all and gave her the courage she afterwards showed was that he put the whole thing to her as a favour, an obligation he should gratefully incur. She figured him as rich, but as fearfully extravagant – saw him all in a glow of high fashion, of good looks, of expensive habits, of charming ways with women. He had for his town residence a big house filled with the spoils of travel and the trophies of the chase; but it was to his country home, an old family place in Essex, that he wished her immediately to proceed.

He had been left, by the death of his parents in India, guardian to a small nephew and a small niece, children of a younger, a military brother whom he had lost two years before. These children were, by the strangest of chances for a man in his position – a lone man without the right sort of experience or a grain of patience – very heavy on his hands. It had all been a great worry and, on his own part doubtless, a series of blunders, but he immensely pitied the poor chicks and had done all he could; had in particular sent them down to his other house, the proper place for them being of course the country, and kept them there from the first with the best people he could find to look after them, parting even with his own servants to wait on them and going down himself, whenever he might, to see how they were doing. The awkward thing was that they had practically no other relations and that his own affairs took up all his time. He had put them in possession of Bly, which was healthy and secure, and had placed at the head of their little establishment – but belowstairs only – an excellent woman, Mrs. Grose, whom he was sure his visitor would like and who had formerly been maid to his mother. She was now housekeeper and was also acting for the time as superintendent to the little girl, of whom, without children of her own, she was by good luck extremely fond. There were plenty of people to help, but of course the young lady who should go down as governess would be in supreme authority. She would also have, in holidays, to look after the small boy, who had been for a term at school – young as he was to be sent, but what else could be done? – and who, as the holidays were about to begin, would be back from one day to the other. There had been for the two children at first a young lady whom they had had the misfortune to lose. She had done for them quite beautifully – she was a most respectable person – till her death, the great awkwardness of which had, precisely, left no alternative but the school for little Miles. Mrs. Grose, since then, in the way of manners and things, had done as she could for Flora; and there were, further, a cook, a housemaid, a dairywoman, an old pony, an old groom and an old gardener, all likewise thoroughly respectable.

So far had Douglas presented his picture when some one put a question. 'And what did the former governess die of? Of so much respectability?'

Our friend's answer was prompt. 'That will come out. I don't anticipate.'

'Pardon me – I thought that was just what you *are* doing.'

'In her successor's place,' I suggested, 'I should have wished to learn if the office brought with it—'

'Necessary danger to life?' Douglas completed my thought. 'She did wish to learn, and she did learn. You shall hear to-morrow what she learnt. Meanwhile of course the prospect struck her as slightly grim. She was young, untried, nervous: it was a vision of serious duties and little company, of really great loneliness. She hesitated – took a couple of days to consult and consider. But the salary offered much exceeded her modest measure, and on a second interview she faced the music, she engaged.' And Douglas, with this, made a pause that, for the benefit of the company, moved me to throw in—

'The moral of which was of course the seduction exercised by the splendid young man. She succumbed to it.'

He got up and, as he had done the night before, went to the fire, gave a stir to a log with his foot, then stood a moment with his back to us. 'She saw him only twice.'

'Yes, but that's just the beauty of her passion.'

A little to my surprise, on this, Douglas turned round to me. 'It *was* the beauty of it. There were others,' he went on, 'who hadn't succumbed. He told her frankly all his difficulty – that for several applicants the conditions had been prohibitive. They were somehow simply afraid. It sounded dull – it sounded strange; and all the more so because of his main condition.'

'Which was—?'

'That she should never trouble him – but never, never: neither appeal nor complain nor write about anything; only meet all questions herself, receive all moneys from his solicitor, take the whole thing over and let him alone. She promised to do this, and she mentioned to me that when, for a moment, disburdened, delighted, he held her hand, thanking her for the sacrifice, she already felt rewarded.'

'But was that all her reward?' one of the ladies asked.

'She never saw him again.'

'Oh!' said the lady; which, as our friend immediately again left us, was the only other word of importance contributed to the subject till, the next night, by the corner of the hearth, in the best chair, he opened the faded red cover of a thin old-fashioned gilt-edged album. The whole thing took indeed more nights than one, but on the first occasion the same lady put another question. 'What's your title?'

'I haven't one.'

'Oh *I* have!' I said. But Douglas, without heeding me, had begun to read with a fine clearness that was like a rendering to the ear of the beauty of his author's hand.

I

I remember the whole beginning as a succession of flights and drops, a little see-saw of the right throbs and the wrong. After rising, in town, to meet his appeal I had at all events a couple of very bad days – found all my doubts bristle again, felt indeed sure I had made a mistake. In this state of mind I spent the long hours of bumping swinging coach that carried me to the stopping-place at which I was to be met by a vehicle from the house. This convenience, I was told, had been ordered, and I found, toward the close of the June afternoon, a commodious fly[1] in waiting for me. Driving at that hour, on a lovely day, through a country the summer sweetness of which served as a friendly welcome, my fortitude revived and, as we turned into the avenue, took a flight that was probably but a proof of the point to which it had sunk. I suppose I had expected, or had dreaded, something so dreary that what greeted me was a good surprise. I remember as a thoroughly pleasant impression the broad clear front, its open windows and fresh curtains and the pair of maids looking out; I remember the lawn and the bright flowers and the crunch of my wheels on the gravel and the clustered tree-tops over which the rooks circled and cawed in the golden sky. The scene had a greatness that made it a different affair from my own scant home, and there immediately appeared at the door, with a little girl in her hand, a civil person who dropped me as decent a curtsey as if I had been the mistress or a distinguished visitor. I had received in Harley Street a narrower notion of the place, and that, as I recalled it, made me think the proprietor still more of a gentleman, suggested that what I was to enjoy might be a matter beyond his promise.

I had no drop again till the next day, for I was carried triumphantly through the following hours by my introduction to the younger of my pupils. The little girl who accompanied Mrs. Grose affected me on the spot as a creature too charming not to make it a great fortune to have to do with her. She was the most beautiful child I had ever seen, and I afterwards wondered why my employer hadn't made more of a point to me of this. I slept little that night – I was too much excited; and this astonished me too, I recollect, remained with me, adding to my sense of the liberality with which I was treated. The large impressive room, one of the best in the house, the great state bed, as I almost felt it, the figured full draperies, the long glasses in which, for the first time, I could see myself from head to foot, all struck me – like the wonderful appeal of my small charge – as so many things thrown in. It was thrown in as well, from the first moment, that I should get on with Mrs. Grose in a relation over which, on my way, in the coach, I fear I had rather brooded. The one appearance indeed that in this early outlook might have made me shrink again was that of her being so inordinately glad to see me. I felt within half an hour that she was so glad – stout simple plain clean wholesome woman – as to be positively on her guard against showing it too much. I wondered even then a little why she should wish *not* to show it, and that, with reflexion, with suspicion, might of course have made me uneasy.

But it was a comfort that there could be no uneasiness in a connexion with anything so beatific as the radiant image of my little girl, the vision of whose angelic beauty had probably more than anything else to do with the restlessness that, before morning, made me several times rise and wander about my room to take in the whole picture and prospect; to watch from my open window the faint summer dawn, to look at such stretches of the rest of the house as I could catch, and to listen, while in the fading dusk the first birds began to twitter, for the possible recurrence of a sound or two, less natural and not without but within, that I had fancied I heard. There had been a moment when I believed I recognized, faint and far, the cry of a child; there had been another when I found myself just consciously starting as at the passage, before my door, of a light footstep. But these fancies were not marked enough not to be thrown off, and it is only in the light, or the gloom, I should rather say, of other and subsequent matters that they now come back to me. To watch, teach, 'form' little Flora would too evidently be the making of a happy and useful life. It had been agreed between us downstairs that after this first occasion I should have her as a matter of course at night, her small white bed being already arranged, to that end, in my room. What I had undertaken was the whole care of her, and she had remained just this last time with Mrs. Grose only as an effect of our consideration for my inevitable strangeness and her natural timidity. In spite of this timidity – which the child herself, in the oddest way in the world, had been perfectly frank and brave about, allowing it, without a sign of uncomfortable consciousness, with the deep sweet serenity indeed of one of Raphael's holy infants,[2] to be discussed, to be imputed to her and to determine us – I felt quite sure she would presently like me. It was part of what I already like Mrs. Grose herself for, the pleasure I could see her feel in my admiration and wonder as I sat at supper with four tall candles and with my pupil, in a high chair and a bib, brightly facing me between them over bread and milk. There were naturally things that in Flora's presence could pass between us only as prodigious and gratified looks, obscure and round-about allusions.

'And the little boy – does he look like her? Is he too so very remarkable?'

One wouldn't, it was already conveyed between us, too grossly flatter a child. 'Oh Miss, *most* remarkable. If you think well of this one!' – and she stood there with a plate in her hand, beaming at our companion, who looked from one of us to the other with placid heavenly eyes that contained nothing to check us.

'Yes; if I do—?'

'You *will* be carried away by the little gentleman!'

'Well, that, I think, is what I came for – to be carried away. I'm afraid, however,' I remember feeling the impulse to add, 'I'm rather easily carried away. I was carried away in London!'

I can still see Mrs. Grose's broad face as she took this in. 'In Harley Street?'

'In Harley Street.'

'Well, Miss, you're not the first – and you won't be the last.'

'Oh I've no pretensions,' I could laugh, 'to being the only one. My other pupil, at any rate, as I understand, comes back to-morrow?'

'Not to-morrow – Friday, Miss. He arrives, as you did, by the coach, under care of the guard, and is to be met by the same carriage.'

I forthwith wanted to know if the proper as well as the pleasant and friendly thing wouldn't therefore be that on the arrival of the public conveyance I should await him with his little sister; a proposition to which Mrs. Grose assented so heartily that I somehow took her manner as a kind of comforting pledge – never falsified, thank heaven! – that we should on every question be quite at one. Oh she was glad I was there!

What I felt the next day was, I suppose, nothing that could be fairly called a reaction from the cheer of my arrival; it was probably at the most only a slight oppression produced by a fuller measure of the scale, as I walked round them, gazed up at them, took them in, of my new circumstances. They had, as it were, an extent and mass for which I had not been prepared and in the presence of which I found myself, freshly, a little scared not less than a little proud. Regular lessons, in this agitation, certainly suffered some wrong; I reflected that my first duty was, by the gentlest arts I could contrive, to win the child into the sense of knowing me. I spent the day with her out of doors; I arranged with her, to her great satisfaction, that it should be she, she only, who might show me the place. She showed it step by step and room by room and secret by secret, with droll delightful childish talk about it and with the result, in half an hour, of our becoming tremendous friends. Young as she was I was struck, throughout our little tour, with her confidence and courage, with the way, in empty chambers and dull corridors, on crooked staircases that made me pause and even on the summit of an old machicolated square tower that made me dizzy, her morning music, her disposition to tell me so many more things than she asked, rang out and led me on. I have not seen Bly since the day I left it, and I dare say that to my present older and more informed eyes it would show a very reduced importance. But as my little conductress, with her hair of gold and her frock of blue, danced before me round corners and pattered down passages, I had the view of a castle of romance inhabited by a rosy sprite, such a place as would somehow, for diversion of the young idea, take all colour out of story-books and fairy-tales. Wasn't it just a story-book over which I had fallen a-doze and a-dream? No; it was a big ugly antique but convenient house, embodying a few features of a building still older, half-displaced and half-utilized, in which I had the fancy of our being almost as lost as a handful of passengers in a great drifting ship. Well, I was strangely at the helm!

II

This came home to me when, two days later, I drove over with Flora to meet, as Mrs. Grose said, the little gentleman; and all the more for an incident that, presenting itself the second evening, had deeply disconcerted me. The first day had been, on the whole, as I have expressed, reassuring; but I was to see it wind up to a change of note. The postbag that evening – it came late – contained a letter for me which, however, in the hand of my employer, I found to be composed but of a few words enclosing another, addressed to himself, with a seal still unbroken. 'This, I recognize, is from the head-master, and the head-master's an awful bore. Read him, please; deal with him; but mind you don't report. Not a word. I'm off!' I broke the seal with a great effort – so great a one that I was a long time coming to it; took the unopened missive at last up to my room and only attacked it just before going to bed. I had better have let it wait till morning, for it gave me a second sleepless night. With no counsel to take, the next day, I was full of distress; and it finally got so the better of me that I determined to open myself at least to Mrs. Grose.

'What does it mean? The child's dismissed his school.'

She gave me a look that I remarked at the moment; then, visibly, with a quick blankness, seemed to try to take it back. 'But aren't they all—?'

'Sent home – yes. But only for the holidays. Miles may never go back at all.'

Consciously, under my attention, she reddened. 'They won't take him?'

'They absolutely decline.'

At this she raised her eyes, which she had turned from me; I saw them fill with good tears. 'What has he done?'

I cast about; then I judged best simply to hand her my document – which, however, had the effect of making her, without taking it, simply put her hands behind her. She shook her head sadly. 'Such things are not for me, Miss.'

My counsellor couldn't read! I winced at my mistake, which I attenuated as I could, and opened the letter again to repeat it to her; then, faltering in the act and folding it up once more, I put it back in my pocket. 'Is he really *bad*?'

The tears were still in her eyes. 'Do the gentlemen say so?'

'They go into no particulars. They simply express their regret that it should be impossible to keep him. That can have but one meaning.' Mrs. Grose listened with dumb emotion; she forbore to ask me what this meaning might be; so that, presently, to put the thing with some coherence and with the mere aid of her presence to my own mind, I went on: 'That he's an injury to the others.'

At this, with one of the quick turns of simple folk, she suddenly flamed up. 'Master Miles! – *him* an injury?'

There was such a flood of good faith in it that, though I had not yet seen the child, my very fears made me jump to the absurdity of the idea. I found myself, to meet my friend the better, offering it, on the spot, sarcastically. 'To his poor little innocent mates!'

'It's too dreadful,' cried Mrs. Grose, 'to say such cruel things! Why he's scarce ten years old.'

'Yes, yes; it would be incredible.'

She was evidently grateful for such a profession. 'See him, Miss, first. *Then* believe it!' I felt forthwith a new impatience to see him; it was the beginning of a curiosity that, all the next hours, was to deepen almost to pain. Mrs. Grose was aware, I could judge, of what she had produced in me, and she followed it up with assurance. 'You might as well believe it of the little lady. Bless her,' she added the next moment – '*look* at her!'

I turned and saw that Flora, whom, ten minutes before, I had established in the schoolroom with a sheet of white paper, a pencil and a copy of nice 'round O's', now presented herself to view at the open door. She expressed in her little way an extraordinary detachment from disagreeable duties, looking at me, however, with a great childish light that seemed to offer it as a mere result of the affection she had conceived for my person, which had rendered necessary that she should follow me. I needed nothing more than this to feel the full force of Mrs. Grose's comparison, and, catching my pupil in my arms, covered her with kisses in which there was a sob of atonement.

None the less, the rest of the day, I watched for further occasion to approach my colleague, especially as, toward evening, I began to fancy she rather sought to avoid me. I overtook her, I remember, on the staircase; we went down together and at the bottom I detained her, holding her there with a hand on her arm. 'I take what you said to me at noon as a declaration that *you've* never known him to be bad.'

She threw back her head; she had clearly by this time, and very honestly, adopted an attitude. 'Oh never known him – I don't pretend *that*!'

I was upset again. 'Then you *have* known him—?'

'Yes indeed, Miss, thank God!'

On reflexion I accepted this. 'You mean that a boy who never is—?'

'Is no boy for *me*!'

I held her tighter. 'You like them with the spirit to be naughty?' Then, keeping pace with her answer, 'So do I!' I eagerly brought out. 'But not to the degree to contaminate—'

'To contaminate?' – my big word left her at a loss.

I explained it. 'To corrupt.'

She stared, taking my meaning in; but it produced in her an odd laugh. 'Are you afraid he'll corrupt *you*?' She put the question with such a fine bold humour that with a laugh, a little silly doubtless, to match her own, I gave way for the time to the apprehension of ridicule.

But the next day, as the hour for my drive approached, I cropped up in another place. 'What was the lady who was here before?'

'The last governess? She was also young and pretty – almost as young and almost as pretty, Miss, even as you.'

'Ah then I hope her youth and her beauty helped her!' I recollect throwing off. 'He seems to like us young and pretty!'

'Oh he *did*,' Mrs. Grose assented: 'it was the way he liked every one!' She had no sooner spoken indeed than she caught herself up. 'I mean that's *his* way – the master's.'

I was struck. 'But of whom did you speak first?'

She looked blank, but she coloured. 'Why of *him*.'

'Of the master?'

'Of who else?'

There was so obviously no one else that the next moment I had lost my impression of her having accidentally said more than she meant; and I merely asked what I wanted to know. 'Did *she* see anything in the boy—?'

'That wasn't right? She never told me.'

I had a scruple, but I overcame it. 'Was she careful – particular?'

Mrs. Grose appeared to try to be conscientious. 'About some things – yes.'

'But not about all?'

Again she considered. 'Well, Miss – she's gone. I won't tell tales.'

'I quite understand your feeling,' I hastened to reply; but I thought it after an instant not opposed to this concession to pursue: 'Did she die here?'

'No – she went off.'

I don't know what there was in this brevity of Mrs. Grose's that struck me as ambiguous. 'Went off to die?' Mrs. Grose looked straight out of the window, but I felt that, hypothetically, I had a right to know what young persons engaged for Bly were expected to do. 'She was taken ill, you mean, and went home?'

'She was not taken ill, so far as appeared, in this house. She left it, at the end of the year, to go home, as she said, for a short holiday, to which the time she had put in had certainly given her a right. We had then a young woman – a nursemaid who had stayed on and who was a good girl and clever; and *she* took the children altogether for the interval. But our young lady never came back, and at the very moment I was expecting her I heard from the master that she was dead.'

I turned this over. 'But of what?'

'He never told me! But please, Miss,' said Mrs. Grose, 'I must get to my work.'

III

Her thus turning her back on me was fortunately not, for my just preoccupations, a snub that could check the growth of our mutual esteem. We met, after I had brought home little Miles, more intimately than ever on the ground of my stupefaction, my general emotion: so monstrous was I then ready to pronounce it that such a child as had now been revealed to me should be under an interdict. I was a little late on the scene of his arrival, and I felt, as he stood wistfully looking out for me before the door of the inn at which the coach had put him down, that I had seen him on the instant, without and within, in the great glow of freshness, the same positive fragrance of purity, in which I had from the first moment seen his little sister. He was incredibly beautiful, and Mrs. Grose had put her finger on it: everything but a sort of passion of tenderness for him was swept away by his presence. What I then and there took him to my heart for was something divine that I have never found to the same degree in any child – his indescribable little air of knowing nothing in the world but love. It would have been impossible to carry a bad name with a greater sweetness of innocence, and by the time I had got back to Bly with him I remained merely bewildered – so far, that is, as I was not outraged – by the sense of the horrible letter locked up in one of the drawers of my room. As soon as I could compass a private word with Mrs. Grose I declared to her that it was grotesque.

She promptly understood me. 'You mean the cruel charge—?'

'It doesn't live an instant. My dear woman, *look* at him!'

She smiled at my pretension to have discovered his charm. 'I assure you, Miss, I do nothing else! What will you say then?' she immediately added.

'In answer to the letter?' I had made up my mind. 'Nothing at all.'

'And to his uncle?'

I was incisive. 'Nothing at all.'

'And to the boy himself?'

I was wonderful. 'Nothing at all.'

She gave with her apron a great wipe to her mouth. 'Then I'll stand by you. We'll see it out.'

'We'll see it out!' I ardently echoed, giving her my hand to make it a vow.

She held me there a moment, then whisked up her apron again with her detached hand. 'Would you mind, Miss, if I used the freedom—'

'To kiss me? No!' I took the good creature in my arms and after we had embraced like sisters felt still more fortified and indignant.

This at all events was for the time: a time so full that as I recall the way it went it reminds me of all the art I now need to make it a little distinct. What I look back at with amazement is the situation I accepted. I had undertaken, with my companion, to see it out, and I was under a charm apparently that could smooth away the extent and the far and difficult connexions of such an effort. I was lifted aloft on a great wave of infatuation and pity. I found it simple, in my ignorance, my confusion and perhaps my conceit, to assume that I could deal with a boy whose education for the world was all on the point of beginning. I am unable even to remember at this day what proposal I framed for the end of his holidays and the resumption of his studies. Lessons with me indeed, that charming summer, we all had a theory that he was to have; but I now feel that for weeks the lessons must have been rather my own. I learnt something – at first certainly – that had not been one of the teachings of my small smothered life; learnt to be amused, and even amusing, and not to think for the morrow. It was the first time, in a manner, that I had known space and air and freedom, all the music of summer and all the mystery of nature. And then there was consideration – and consideration was sweet. Oh it was a trap – not designed but deep – to my imagination, to my delicacy, perhaps to my vanity;

to whatever in me was most excitable. The best way to picture it all is to say that I was off my guard. They gave me so little trouble – they were of a gentleness so extraordinary. I used to speculate – but even this with a dim disconnectedness – as to how the rough future (for all futures are rough!) would handle them and might bruise them. They had the bloom of health and happiness; and yet, as if I had been in charge of a pair of little grandees, of princes of the blood, for whom everything, to be right, would have to be fenced about and ordered and arranged, the only form that in my fancy the after-years could take for them was that of a romantic, a really royal extension of the garden and the park. It may be of course above all that what suddenly broke into this gives the previous time a charm of stillness – that hush in which something gathers or crouches. The change was actually like the spring of a beast.

In the first weeks the days were long; they often, at their finest, gave me what I used to call my own hour, the hour when, for my pupils, tea-time and bed-time having come and gone, I had before my final retirement a small interval alone. Much as I liked my companions this hour was the thing in the day I liked most; and I liked it best of all when, as the light faded – or rather, I should say, the day lingered and the last calls of the last birds sounded, in a flushed sky, from the old trees – I could take a turn into the grounds and enjoy, almost with a sense of property that amused and flattered me, the beauty and dignity of the place. It was a pleasure at these moments to feel myself tranquil and justified; doubtless perhaps also to reflect that by my discretion, my quiet good sense and general high propriety, I was giving pleasure – if he ever thought of it! – to the person to whose pressure I had yielded. What I was doing was what he had earnestly hoped and directly asked of me, and that I *could*, after all, do it proved even a greater joy than I had expected. I dare say I fancied myself in short a remarkable young woman and took comfort in the faith that this would more publicly appear. Well, I needed to be remarkable to offer a front to the remarkable things that presently gave their first sign.

It was plump, one afternoon, in the middle of my very hour: the children were tucked away and I had come out for my stroll.

One of the thoughts that, as I don't in the least shrink now from noting, used to be with me in these wanderings was that it would be as charming as a charming story suddenly to meet some one. Some one would appear there at the turn of a path and would stand before me and smile and approve. I didn't ask more than that – I only asked that he should *know*; and the only way to be sure he knew would be to see it, and the kind light of it, in his handsome face. That was exactly present to me – by which I mean the face was – when, on the first of these occasions, at the end of a long June day, I stopped short on emerging from one of the plantations and coming into view of the house. What arrested me on the spot – and with a shock much greater than any vision had allowed for – was the sense that my imagination had, in a flash, turned real. He did stand there! – but high up, beyond the lawn and at the very top of the tower to which, on that first morning, little Flora had conducted me. This tower was one of a pair – square incongruous crenellated structures – that were distinguished, for some reason, though I could see little difference, as the new and the old. They flanked opposite ends of the house and were probably architectural absurdities, redeemed in a measure indeed by not being wholly disengaged nor of a height too pretentious, dating, in their gingerbread antiquity, from a romantic revival that was already a respectable past. I admired them, had fancies about them, for we could all profit in a degree, especially when they loomed through the dusk, by the grandeur of their actual battlements; yet it was not at such an elevation that the figure I had so often invoked seemed most in place.

It produced in me, this figure, in the clear twilight, I remember, two distinct gasps of emotion, which were, sharply, the shock of my first and that of my second surprise. My second was a violent perception of the mistake of my first: the man who met my eyes was not the person I had precipitately supposed. There came to me thus a bewilderment of vision of which, after these years, there is no living view that I can hope to give. An unknown man in a lonely place is a permitted object of fear to a young woman privately bred; and the figure that faced me was – a few more seconds assured me – as little any one else I knew as it was the image that had been in my mind. I had not seen it in Harley Street – I had not seen it anywhere. The place moreover, in the strangest way in the world, had on the instant and by the very fact of its appearance become a solitude. To me at least, making my statement here with a deliberation with which I have never made it, the whole feeling of the moment returns. It was as if, while I took in, what I did take in, all the rest of the scene had been stricken with death. I can hear again, as I write, the intense hush in which the sounds of evening dropped. The rooks stopped cawing in the golden sky and the friendly hour lost for the unspeakable minute all its voice. But there was no other change in nature, unless indeed it were a change that I saw with a stranger sharpness. The gold was still in the sky, the clearness in the air, and the man who looked at me over the battlements was as definite as a picture in a frame. That's how I thought, with extraordinary quickness, of each person he might have been and that he wasn't. We were confronted across our distance quite long enough for me to ask myself with intensity who then he was and to feel, as an effect of my inability to say, a wonder that in a few seconds more became intense.

The great question, or one of these, is afterwards, I know, with regard to certain matters, the question of how long they have lasted. Well, this matter of mine, think what you will of it, lasted while I caught at a dozen possibilities, none of which made a difference for the better, that I could see, in there having been in the house – and for how long, above all? – a person of whom I was in ignorance. It lasted while I just bridled a little with the sense of how my office seemed to require that there should be no such ignorance and no such person. It lasted while this visitant, at all events – and there was a touch of the strange freedom, as I remember, in the sign of familiarity of his wearing no hat – seemed to fix me, from his position, with just the question, just the scrutiny through the fading light, that his own presence provoked. We were too far apart to call to each other, but there was a moment at which, at shorter range, some challenge between us, breaking the hush, would have been the right result of our straight mutual stare. He was in one of the angles, the one away from the house, very erect, as it struck me, and with both hands on the ledge. So I saw him as I see the letters I form on this page; then, exactly, after a minute, as if to add to the spectacle, he slowly changed his place – passed, looking at me hard all the while, to the opposite corner of the platform. Yes, it was intense to me that during this transit he never took his eyes from me, and I can see at this moment the way his hand, as he went, moved from one of the crenellations to the next. He stopped at the other corner, but less long, and even as he turned away still markedly fixed me. He turned away; that was all I knew.

IV

It was not that I didn't wait, on this occasion, for more, since I was as deeply rooted as shaken. Was there a 'secret' at Bly – a mystery of Udolpho or an insane, an unmentionable relative kept in unsuspected confinement?[1] I can't say how long I turned it over, or how long, in confusion of curiosity and dread, I remained where I had had my collision; I only recall that when I re-entered the house darkness had quite closed in. Agitation, in the interval, certainly had held me and driven me, for I must, in circling about the place, have walked three miles; but I was to be later on so much more overwhelmed that this mere dawn of alarm was a comparatively human chill. The most singular part of it in fact – singular as the rest had been – was the part I became, in the hall, aware of in meeting Mrs. Grose. This picture comes back to me in the general train – the impression, as I received it on my return, of the wide white panelled space, bright in the lamplight and with its portraits and red carpet, and of the good surprised look of my friend, which immediately told me she had missed me. It came to me straightway, under her contact, that, with plain heartiness, mere relieved anxiety at my appearance, she knew nothing whatever that could bear upon the incident I had there ready for her. I had not suspected in advance that her comfortable face would pull me up, and I somehow measured the importance of what I had seen by my thus finding myself hesitate to mention it. Scarce anything in the whole history seems to me so odd as this fact that my real beginning of fear was one, as I may say, with the instinct of sparing my companion. On the spot, accordingly, in the pleasant hall and with her eyes on me, I, for a reason that I couldn't then have phrased, achieved an inward revolution – offered a vague pretext for my lateness and, with the plea of the beauty of the night and of the heavy dew and wet feet, went as soon as possible to my room.

Here it was another affair; here, for many days after, it was a queer affair enough. There were hours, from day to day – or at least there were moments, snatched even from clear duties – when I had to shut myself up to think. It wasn't so much yet that I was more nervous than I could bear to be as that I was remarkably afraid of becoming so; for the truth I had now to turn over was simply and clearly the truth that I could arrive at no account whatever of the visitor with whom I had been so inexplicably and yet, as it seemed to me, so intimately concerned. It took me little time to see that I might easily sound, without forms of enquiry and without exciting remark, any domestic complication. The shock I had suffered must have sharpened all my senses; I felt sure, at the end of three days and as the result of mere closer attention, that I had not been practised upon by the servants nor made the object of any 'game'. Of whatever it was that I knew nothing was known around me. There was but one sane inference: some one had taken a liberty rather monstrous. That was what, repeatedly, I dipped into my room and locked the door to say to myself. We had been, collectively, subject to an intrusion; some unscrupulous traveller, curious in old houses, had made his way in unobserved, enjoyed the prospect from the best point of view and then stolen out as he came. If he had given me such a bold hard stare, that was but a part of his indiscretion. The good thing, after all, was that we should surely see no more of him.

This was not so good a thing, I admit, as not to leave me to judge that what, essentially, made nothing else much signify was simply my charming work. My charming work was just my life with Miles and Flora, and through nothing could I so like it as through feeling that to throw myself into it was to throw myself out of my trouble. The attraction of my small charges was a constant joy, leading me to wonder afresh at the vanity of my original fears, the distaste I had begun by entertaining for the probable grey prose of my office. There was to be no grey prose, it appeared, and no long grind; so how could work not be charming that presented itself as daily beauty? It was all the romance of the nursery and the poetry of the schoolroom. I don't mean by this of course that we studied only fiction and verse; I mean that I can express no otherwise the sort of interest my companions inspired. How can I describe that except by saying that instead of growing deadly used to them – and it's a marvel for a governess: I call the sisterhood to witness! – I made constant fresh discoveries. There was one direction, assuredly, in which these discoveries stopped: deep obscurity continued to cover the region of the boy's conduct at school. It had been promptly given me, I have noted, to face that mystery without a pang. Perhaps even it would be nearer the truth to say that – without a word – he himself had cleared it up. He had made the whole charge absurd. My conclusion bloomed there with the real rose-flush of his innocence: he was only too fine and fair for the little horrid unclean school-world, and he had paid a price for it. I reflected acutely that the sense of such individual differences, such superiorities of quality, always, on the part of the majority – which could include even stupid sordid head-masters – turns infallibly to the vindictive.

Both the children had a gentleness – it was their only fault, and it never made Miles a muff – that kept them (how shall I express it?) almost impersonal and certainly quite unpunishable. They were like those cherubs of the anecdote who had – morally at any rate – nothing to whack! I remember feeling with Miles in especial as if he had had, as it were, nothing to call even an infinitesimal history. We expect of a small child scant enough 'antecedents', but there was in this beautiful little boy something extraordinarily sensitive, yet extraordinarily happy, that, more than in any creature of his age I have seen, struck me as beginning anew each day. He had never for a second suffered. I took this as a direct disproof of his having really been chastised. If he had been wicked he would have 'caught' it, and I should have caught it by the rebound – I should have found the trace, should have felt the wound and the dishonour.[2] I could reconstitute nothing at all, and he was therefore an angel. He never spoke of his school, never mentioned a comrade or a master; and I, for my part, was quite too much disgusted to allude to them. Of course I was under the spell, and the wonderful part is that, even at the time, I perfectly knew I was. But I gave myself up to it; it was an antidote to any pain, and I had more pains than one. I was in receipt in these days of disturbing letters from home, where things were not going well. But with this joy of my children what things in the world mattered? That was the question I used to put to my scrappy retirements. I was dazzled by their loveliness.

There was a Sunday – to get on – when it rained with such force and for so many hours that there could be no procession to church; in consequence of which, as the day declined, I had arranged with Mrs. Grose that, should the evening show improvement, we would attend together the late service. The rain happily stopped, and I prepared for our walk, which, through the park and by the good road to the village, would be a matter of twenty minutes. Coming downstairs to meet my colleague in the hall, I remembered a pair of gloves that had required three stitches and that had received them – with a publicity perhaps not edifying – while I sat with the children at their tea, served on Sundays, by exception, in that cold clean temple of mahogany and brass, the 'grown-up' dining-room. The gloves had been dropped there, and I turned in to recover them. The day was grey enough, but the afternoon light still lingered, and it enabled me, on crossing the threshold, not only to recognize, on a chair near the wide window, then closed, the articles I wanted, but to become aware of a person on the other side of the window and looking straight in. One step into the room had sufficed; my vision was instantaneous; it was all there. The person looking straight in was the person who had already appeared to me. He appeared thus again with I won't say greater distinctness, for that was impossible, but with a nearness that represented a forward stride in our intercourse and made me, as I met him, catch my breath and turn cold. He was the same – he was the same, and seen, this time, as he had been seen before, from the waist up, the window, though the dining-room was on the ground floor, not going down to the terrace on which he stood. His face was close to the glass, yet the effect of this better view was, strangely, just to show me how intense the former had been. He remained but a few seconds – long enough to convince me he also saw and recognized; but it was as if I had been looking at him for years and had known him always. Something, however, happened this time that had not happened before; his stare into my face, through the glass and across the room, was as deep and hard as then, but it quitted me for a moment during which I could still watch it, see it fix successively several other things. On the spot there came to me the added shock of a certitude that it was not for me he had come. He had come for some one else.

The flash of this knowledge – for it was knowledge in the midst of dread – produced in me the most extraordinary effect, starting, as I stood there, a sudden vibration of duty and courage. I say courage because I was beyond all doubt already far gone. I bounded straight out of the door again, reached that of the house, got in an instant upon the drive and, passing along the terrace as fast as I could rush, turned a corner and came full in sight. But it was in sight of nothing now – my visitor had vanished. I stopped, almost dropped, with the real relief of this; but I took in the whole scene – I gave him time to reappear. I call it time, but how long was it? I can't speak to the purpose to-day of the duration of these things. That kind of measure must have left me: they couldn't have lasted as they actually appeared to me to last. The terrace and the whole place, the lawn and the garden beyond it, all I could see of the park, were empty with a great emptiness. There were shrubberies and big trees, but I remember the clear assurance I felt that none of them concealed him. He was there or was not there: not there if I didn't see him. I got hold of this; then, instinctively, instead of returning as I had come, went to the window. It was confusedly present to me that I ought to place myself where he had stood. I did so; I applied my face to the pane and looked, as he had looked, into the room. As if, at this moment, to show me exactly what his range had been, Mrs. Grose, as I had done for himself just before, came in from the hall. With this I had the full image of a repetition of what had already occurred. She saw me as I had seen my own visitant; she pulled up short as I had done; I gave her something of the shock that I had received. She turned white, and this made me ask myself if I had blanched as much. She stared, in short, and retreated just on *my* lines, and I knew she had then passed out and come round to me and that I should presently meet her. I remained where I was, and while I waited I thought of more things than one. But there's only one I take space to mention. I wondered why *she* should be scared.

V

Oh she let me know as soon as, round the corner of the house, she loomed again into view. 'What in the name of goodness is the matter—?' She was now flushed and out of breath.

I said nothing till she came quite near. 'With me?' I must have made a wonderful face. 'Do I show it?'

'You're as white as a sheet. You look awful.'

I considered; I could meet on this, without scruple, any degree of innocence. My need to respect the bloom of Mrs. Grose's had dropped, without a rustle, from my shoulders, and if I wavered for the instant it was not with what I kept back. I put out my hand to her and she took it; I held her hard a little, liking to feel her close to me. There was a kind of support in the shy heave of her surprise. 'You came for me for church, of course, but I can't go.'

'Has anything happened?'

'Yes. You must know now. Did I look very queer?'

'Through this window? Dreadful!'

'Well,' I said, 'I've been frightened.' Mrs. Grose's eyes expressed plainly that *she* had no wish to be, yet also that she knew too well her place not to be ready to share with me any marked inconvenience. Oh it was quite settled that she *must* share! 'Just what you saw from the dining-room a minute ago was the effect of that. What *I* saw – just before – was much worse.'

Her hand tightened. 'What was it?'

'An extraordinary man. Looking in.'

'What extraordinary man?'

'I haven't the least idea.'

Mrs. Grose gazed round us in vain. 'Then where is he gone?'

'I know still less.'

'Have you seen him before?'

'Yes – once. On the old tower.'

She could only look at me harder. 'Do you mean he's a stranger?'

'Oh very much!'

'Yet you didn't tell me?'

'No – for reasons. But now that you've guessed—'

Mrs. Grose's round eyes encountered this charge. 'Ah I haven't guessed!' she said very simply. 'How can I if *you* don't imagine?'

'I don't in the very least.'

'You've seen him nowhere but on the tower?'

'And on this spot just now.'

Mrs. Grose looked round again. 'What was he doing on the tower?'

'Only standing there and looking down at me.'

She thought a minute. 'Was he a gentleman?'

I found I had no need to think. 'No.' She gazed in deeper wonder. 'No.'

'Then nobody about the place? Nobody from the village?'

'Nobody – nobody. I didn't tell you, but I made sure.'

She breathed a vague relief: this was, oddly, so much to the good. It only went indeed a little way. 'But if he isn't a gentleman—'

'What *is* he? He's a horror.'

'A horror?'

'He's – God help me if I know *what* he is!'

Mrs. Grose looked round once more; she fixed her eyes on the duskier distance and then, pulling herself together, turned to me with full inconsequence. 'It's time we should be at church.'

'Oh I'm not fit for church!'

'Won't it do you good?'

'It won't do *them*—!' I nodded at the house.

'The children?'

'I can't leave them now.'

'You're afraid—?'

I spoke boldly. 'I'm afraid of *him*.'

Mrs. Grose's large face showed me, at this, for the first time, the far-away faint glimmer of a consciousness more acute: I somehow made out in it the delayed dawn of an idea I myself had not given her and that was as yet quite obscure to me. It comes back to me that I thought instantly of this as something I could get from her; and I felt it to be connected with the desire she presently showed to know more. 'When was it – on the tower?'

'About the middle of the month. At this same hour.'

'Almost at dark,' said Mrs. Grose.

'Oh no, not nearly. I saw him as I see you.'

'Then how did he get in?'

'And how did he get out?' I laughed. 'I had no opportunity to ask him! This evening, you see,' I pursued, 'he has not been able to get in.'

'He only peeps?'

'I hope it will be confined to that!' She had now let go my hand; she turned away a little. I waited an instant; then I brought out: 'Go to church. Goodbye. I must watch.'

Slowly she faced me again. 'Do you fear for them?'

We met in another long look. 'Don't *you*?' Instead of answering she came nearer to the window and, for a minute, applied her face to the glass. 'You see how he could see,' I meanwhile went on.

She didn't move. 'How long was he here?'

'Till I came out. I came to meet him.'

Mrs. Grose at last turned round, and there was still more in her face. '*I* couldn't have come out.'

'Neither could I!' I laughed again. 'But I did come. I've my duty.'

'So have I mine,' she replied; after which she added: 'What's he like?'

'I've been dying to tell you. But he's like nobody.'

'Nobody?' she echoed.

'He has no hat.' Then seeing in her face that she already, in this, with a deeper dismay, found a touch of picture, I quickly added stroke to stroke. 'He has red hair, very red, close-curling, and a pale face, long in shape, with straight good features and little rather queer whiskers that are as red as his hair. His eyebrows are somehow darker; they look particularly arched and as if they might move a good deal. His eyes are sharp, strange – awfully; but I only know clearly that they're rather small and very fixed. His mouth's wide, and his lips are thin, and except for his little whiskers he's quite clean-shaven. He gives me a sort of sense of looking like an actor.'

'An actor!' It was impossible to resemble one less, at least, than Mrs. Grose at that moment.

'I've never seen one, but so I suppose them. He's tall, active, erect,' I continued, 'but never – no, never! – a gentleman.'

My companion's face had blanched as I went on; her round eyes started and her mild mouth gaped. 'A gentleman?' she gasped, confounded, stupefied: 'a gentleman *he*?'

'You know him then?'

She visibly tried to hold herself. 'But he *is* handsome?'

I saw the way to help her. 'Remarkably!'

'And dressed—?'

'In somebody's clothes. They're smart, but they're not his own.'

She broke into a breathless affirmative groan. 'They're the master's!'

I caught it up. 'You *do* know him?'

She faltered but a second. 'Quint!' she cried.

'Quint?'

'Peter Quint – his own man, his valet, when he was here!'

'When the master was?'

Gaping still, but meeting me, she pieced it all together. 'He never wore his hat, but he did wear – well, there were waistcoats missed! They were both here – last year. Then the master went, and Quint was alone.'

I followed, but halting a little. 'Alone?'

'Alone with *us*.' Then as from a deeper depth, 'In charge,' she added.

'And what became of him?'

She hung fire so long that I was still more mystified. 'He went too,' she brought out at last.

'Went where?'

Her expression, at this, became extraordinary. 'God knows where! He died.'

'Died?' I almost shrieked.

She seemed fairly to square herself, plant herself more firmly to express the wonder of it. 'Yes. Mr. Quint's dead.'

VI

It took of course more than that particular passage to place us together in presence of what we had now to live with as we could, my dreadful liability to impressions of the order so vividly exemplified, and my companion's knowledge henceforth – a knowledge half consternation and half compassion – of that liability. There had been this evening, after the revelation that left me for an hour so prostrate – there had been for either of us no attendance on any service but a little service of tears and vows, of prayers and promises, a climax to the series of mutual challenges and pledges that had straightway ensued on our retreating together to the schoolroom and shutting ourselves up there to have everything out. The result of our having everything out was simply to reduce our situation to the last rigour of its elements. She herself had seen nothing, not the shadow of a shadow, and nobody in the house but the governess was in the governess's plight; yet she accepted without directly impugning my sanity the truth as I gave it to her, and ended by showing me on this ground an awestricken tenderness, a deference to my more than questionable privilege, of which the very breath has remained with me as that of the sweetest of human charities.

What was settled between us accordingly that night was that we thought we might bear things together; and I was not even sure that in spite of her exemption it was she who had the best of the burden. I knew at this hour, I think, as well as I knew later, what I was capable of meeting to shelter my pupils; but it took me some time to be wholly sure of what my honest comrade was prepared for to keep terms with so stiff an agreement. I was queer company enough – quite as queer as the company I received; but as I trace over what we went through I see how much common ground we must have found in the one idea that, by good fortune, *could* steady us: It was the idea, the second movement, that led me straight out, as I may say, of the inner chamber of my dread. I could take the air in the court, at least, and there Mrs. Grose could join me. Perfectly can I recall now the particular way strength came to me before we separated for the night. We had gone over and over every feature of what I had seen.

'He was looking for some one else, you say – some one who was not you?'

'He was looking for little Miles.' A portentous clearness now possessed me. '*That's* whom he was looking for.'

'But how do you know?'

'I know, I know, I know!' My exaltation grew.

'And *you* know, my dear!'

She didn't deny this, but I required, I felt, not even so much telling as that. She took it up again in a moment. 'What if *he* should see him?'

'Little Miles? That's what he wants!'

She looked immensely scared again. 'The child?'

'Heaven forbid! The man. He wants to appear to *them*.' That he might was an awful conception, and yet somehow I could keep it at bay; which moreover, as we lingered there, was what I succeeded in practically proving. I had an absolute certainty that I should see again what I had already seen, but something within me said that by offering myself bravely as the sole subject of such experience, by accepting, by inviting, by surmounting it all, I should serve as an expiatory victim and guard the tranquillity of the rest of the household. The children in especial I should thus fence about and absolutely save. I recall one of the last things I said that night to Mrs. Grose.

'It does strike me that my pupils have never mentioned—!'

She looked at me hard as I musingly pulled up. 'His having been here and the time they were with him?'

'The time they were with him, and his name, his presence, his history, in any way. They've never alluded to it.'

'Oh the little lady doesn't remember. She never heard or knew.'

'The circumstances of his death?' I thought with some intensity. 'Perhaps not. But Miles would remember – Miles would know.'

'Ah don't try him!' broke from Mrs. Grose.

I returned her the look she had given me. 'Don't be afraid.' I continued to think. 'It *is* rather odd.'

'That he has never spoken of him?'

'Never by the least reference. And you tell me they were "great friends".'

'Oh it wasn't *him*!' Mrs. Grose with emphasis declared. 'It was Quint's own fancy. To play with him, I mean – to spoil him.' She paused a moment; then she added: 'Quint was much too free.'

This gave me, straight from my vision of his face – *such* a face! – a sudden sickness of disgust. 'Too free with *my* boy?'

'Too free with every one!'

I forbore for the moment to analyse this description further than by the reflection that a part of it applied to several of the members of the household, of the half-dozen maids and men who were still of our small colony. But there was everything, for our apprehension, in the lucky fact that no discomfortable legend, no perturbation of scullions, had ever, within any one's memory, attached to the kind old place. It had neither had name nor ill fame, and Mrs. Grose, most apparently, only desired to cling to me and to quake in silence. I even put her, the very last thing of all, to the test. It was when, at midnight, she had her hand on the schoolroom door to take leave. 'I *have* it from you then – for it's of great importance – that he was definitely and admittedly bad?'

'Oh not admittedly. *I* knew it – but the master didn't.'

'And you never told him?'

'Well, he didn't like tale-bearing – he hated complaints. He was terribly short with anything of that kind, and if people were all right to *him*—'

'He wouldn't be bothered with more?' This squared well enough with my impression of him: he was not a trouble-loving gentleman, nor so very particular perhaps about some of the company he himself kept. All the same, I pressed my informant. 'I promise you *I* would have told!'

She felt my discrimination. 'I dare say I was wrong. But really I was afraid.'

'Afraid of what?'

'Of things that man could do. Quint was so clever – he was so deep.'

I took this in still more than I probably showed. 'You weren't afraid of anything else? Not of his effect—?'

'His effect?' she repeated with a face of anguish and waiting while I faltered.

'On innocent little precious lives. They were in your charge.'

'No, they weren't in mine!' she roundly and distressfully returned. 'The master believed in him and placed him here because he was supposed not to be quite in health and the country air so good for him. So he had everything to say. Yes' – she let me have it – 'even about *them*.'

'Them – that creature?' I had to smother a kind of howl. 'And you could bear it?'

'No. I couldn't – and I can't now!' And the poor woman burst into tears.

A rigid control, from the next day, was, as I have said, to follow them; yet how often and how passionately, for a week, we came back together to the subject! Much as we had discussed it that Sunday night, I was, in the immediate later hours in especial – for it may be imagined whether I slept – still haunted with the shadow of something she had not told me. I myself had kept back nothing, but there was a word Mrs. Grose had kept back. I was sure moreover by morning that this was not from a failure of frankness, but because on every side there were fears. It seems to me indeed, in raking it all over, that by the time the morrow's sun was high I had restlessly read into the facts before us almost all the meaning they were to receive from subsequent and more cruel occurrences. What they gave me above all was just the sinister figure of the living man – the dead one would keep a while! – and of the months he had continuously passed at Bly, which, added up, made a formidable stretch. The limit of this evil time had arrived only when, on the dawn of a winter's morning, Peter Quint was found, by a labourer going to early work, stone dead on the road from the village: a catastrophe explained

– superficially at least – by a visible wound to his head; such a wound as might have been produced (and as, on the final evidence, *had* been) by a fatal slip, in the dark and after leaving the public-house, on the steepish icy slope, a wrong path altogether, at the bottom of which he lay. The icy slope, the turn mistaken at night and in liquor, accounted for much – practically, in the end and after the inquest and boundless chatter, for everything; but there had been matters in his life, strange passages and perils, secret disorders, vices more than suspected, that would have accounted for a good deal more.

I scarce know how to put my story into words that shall be a credible picture of my state of mind; but I was in these days literally able to find a joy in the extraordinary flight of heroism the occasion demanded of me. I now saw that I had been asked for a service admirable and difficult; and there would be a greatness in letting it be seen – oh in the right quarter! – that I could succeed where many another girl might have failed. It was an immense help to me – I confess I rather applaud myself as I look back! – that I saw my response so strongly and so simply. I was there to protect and defend the little creatures in the world the most bereaved and the most loveable, the appeal of whose helplessness had suddenly become only too explicit, a deep constant ache of one's own engaged affection. We were cut off, really, together; we were united in our danger. They had nothing but me, and I – well, I had *them*. It was in short a magnificent chance. This chance presented itself to me in an image richly material. I was a screen – I was to stand before them. The more I saw the less they would. I began to watch them in a stifled suspense, a disguised tension, that might well, had it continued too long, have turned to something like madness. What saved me, as I now see, was that it turned to another matter altogether. It didn't last as suspense – it was superseded by horrible proofs. Proofs, I say, yes – from the moment I really took hold.

This moment dated from an afternoon hour that I happened to spend in the grounds with the younger of my pupils alone. We had left Miles indoors, on the red cushion of a deep window-seat; he had wished to finish a book, and I had been glad to encourage a purpose so laudable in a young man whose only defect was a certain ingenuity of restlessness. His sister, on the contrary, had been alert to come out, and I strolled with her half an hour, seeking the shade, for the sun was still high and the day exceptionally warm. I was aware afresh with her, as we went, of how, like her brother, she contrived – it was the charming thing in both children – to let me alone without appearing to drop me and to accompany me without appearing to oppress. They were never importunate and yet never listless. My attention to them all really went to seeing them amuse themselves immensely without me: this was a spectacle they seemed actively to prepare and that employed me as an active admirer. I walked in a world of their invention – they had no occasion whatever to draw upon mine; so that my time was taken only with being for them some remarkable person or thing that the game of the moment required and that was merely, thanks to my superior, my exalted stamp, a happy and highly distinguished sinecure. I forget what I was on the present occasion; I only remember that I was something very important and very quiet and that Flora was playing very hard. We were on the edge of the lake, and, as we had lately begun geography, the lake was the Sea of Azof.[1]

Suddenly, amid these elements, I became aware that on the other side of the Sea of Azof we had an interested spectator. The way this knowledge gathered in me was the strangest thing in the world – the strangest, that is, except the very much stranger in which it quickly merged itself. I had sat down with a piece of work – for I was something or other that could sit – on the old stone bench which overlooked the pond; and in this position I began to take in with certitude and yet without direct vision the presence, a good way off, of a third person. The old trees, the thick shrubbery, made a great and pleasant shade, but it was all suffused with the brightness of the hot still hour. There was no ambiguity in anything; none whatever at least in the conviction I from one moment to another found myself forming as to what I should see straight before me and across the lake as a consequence of raising my eyes. They were attached at this juncture to the stitching in which I was engaged, and I can feel once more the spasm of my effort not to move them till I should so have steadied myself as to be able to make up my mind what to do.

There was an alien object in view – a figure whose right of presence I instantly and passionately questioned. I recollect counting over perfectly the possibilities, reminding myself that nothing was more natural for instance than the appearance of one of the men about the place, or even of a messenger, a postman or a tradesman's boy, from the village. That reminder had as little effect on my practical certitude as I was conscious – still even without looking – of its having upon the character and attitude of our visitor. Nothing was more natural than that these things should be the other things they absolutely were not.

Of the positive identity of the apparition I would assure myself as soon as the small clock of my courage should have ticked out the right second; meanwhile, with an effort that was already sharp enough, I transferred my eyes straight to little Flora, who, at the moment, was about ten yards away. My heart had stood still for an instant with the wonder and terror of the question whether she too would see; and I held my breath while I waited for what a cry from her, what some sudden innocent sign either of interest or of alarm, would tell me. I waited, but nothing came; then in the first place – and there is something more dire in this, I feel, than in anything I have to relate – I was determined by a sense that within a minute all spontaneous sounds from her had dropped; and in the second by the circumstance that also within the minute she had, in her play, turned her back to the water. This was her attitude when I at last looked at her – looked with the confirmed conviction that we were still, together, under direct personal notice. She had picked up a small flat piece of wood which happened to have in it a little hole that had evidently suggested to her the idea of sticking in another fragment that might figure as a mast and make the thing a boat. This second morsel, as I watched her, she was very markedly and intently attempting to tighten in its place. My apprehension of what she was doing sustained me so that after some seconds I felt I was ready for more. Then I again shifted my eyes – I faced what I had to face.

VII

I got hold of Mrs. Grose as soon after this as I could; and I can give no intelligible account of how I fought out the interval. Yet I still hear myself cry as I fairly threw myself into her arms: 'They *know* – it's too monstrous: they know, they know!'

'And what on earth—?' I felt her incredulity as she held me.

'Why all that *we* know – and heaven knows what more besides!' Then as she released me I made it out to her, made it out perhaps only now with full coherency even to myself. 'Two hours ago, in the garden' – I could scarce articulate – 'Flora *saw*!'

Mrs. Grose took it as she might have taken a blow in the stomach. 'She has told you?' she panted.

'Not a word – that's the horror. She kept it to herself! The child of eight, *that* child!' Unutterable still for me was the stupefaction of it.

Mrs. Grose of course could only gape the wider. 'Then how do you know?'

'I was there – I saw with my eyes: saw she was perfectly aware.'

'Do you mean aware of *him*?'

'No – of *her*.' I was conscious as I spoke that I looked prodigious things, for I got the slow reflexion of them in my companion's face. 'Another person – this time; but a figure of quite as unmistakeable horror and evil: a woman in black, pale and dreadful – with such an air also, and such a face! – on the other side of the lake. I was there with the child – quiet for the hour; and in the midst of it she came.'

'Came how – from where?'

'From where they come from! She just appeared and stood there – but not so near.'

'And without coming nearer?'

'Oh for the effect and the feeling she might have been as close as you!'

My friend, with an odd impulse, fell back a step. 'Was she some one you've never seen?'

'Never. But some one the child has. Some one *you* have.' Then to show how I had thought it all out: 'My predecessor – the one who died.'

'Miss Jessel?'

'Miss Jessel. You don't believe me?' I pressed.

She turned right and left in her distress. 'How can you be sure?'

This drew from me, in the state of my nerves, a flash of impatience. 'Then ask Flora – *she's* sure!' But I had no sooner spoken than I caught myself up. 'No, for God's sake *don't*! She'll say she isn't – she'll lie!'

Mrs. Grose was not too bewildered instinctively to protest. 'Ah how *can* you?'

'Because I'm clear. Flora doesn't want me to know.'

'It's only then to spare you.'

'No, no – there are depths, depths! The more I go over it the more I see in it, and the more I see in it the more I fear. I don't know what I *don't* see, what I *don't* fear!'

Mrs. Grose tried to keep up with me. 'You mean you're afraid of seeing her again?'

'Oh no; that's nothing – now!' Then I explained. 'It's of *not* seeing her.'

But my companion only looked wan. 'I don't understand.'

'Why, it's that the child may keep it up – and that the child assuredly *will* – without my knowing it.'

At the image of this possibility Mrs. Grose for a moment collapsed, yet presently to pull herself together again as from the positive force of the sense of what, should we yield an inch, there would really be to give way to. 'Dear, dear – we must keep our heads! And after all, if she doesn't mind it—!' She even tried a grim joke. 'Perhaps she likes it!'

'Like *such* things – a scrap of an infant!'

'Isn't it just a proof of her blest innocence?' my friend bravely enquired.

She brought me, for the instant, almost round. 'Oh we must clutch at *that* – we must cling to it! If it isn't a proof of what you say, it's a proof of – God knows what! For the woman's a horror of horrors.'

Mrs. Grose, at this, fixed her eyes a minute on the ground; then at last raising them, 'Tell me how you know,' she said.

'Then you admit it's what she was?' I cried.

'Tell me how you know,' my friend simply repeated.

'Know? By seeing her! By the way she looked.'

'At you, do you mean – so wickedly?'

'Dear me, no – I could have borne that. She gave me never a glance. She only fixed the child.'

Mrs. Grose tried to see it. 'Fixed her?'

'Ah with such awful eyes!'

She stared at mine as if they might really have resembled them. 'Do you mean of dislike?'

'God help us, no. Of something much worse.'

'Worse than dislike?' – this left her indeed at a loss.

'With a determination – indescribable. With a kind of fury of intention.'

I made her turn pale. 'Intention?'

'To get hold of her.' Mrs. Grose – her eyes just lingering on mine – gave a shudder and walked to the window; and while she stood there looking out I completed my statement. '*That's* what Flora knows.'

After a little she turned round. 'The person was in black, you say?'

'In mourning – rather poor, almost shabby. But – yes – with extraordinary beauty.' I now recognized to what I had at last, stroke by stroke, brought the victim of my confidence, for she quite visibly weighed this. 'Oh handsome – very, very,' I insisted; 'wonderfully handsome. But infamous.'

She slowly came back to me. 'Miss Jessel – *was* infamous.' She once more took my hand in both her own, holding it as tight as if to fortify me against the increase of alarm I might draw from this disclosure. 'They were both infamous,' she finally said.

So for a little we faced it once more together; and I found absolutely a degree of help in seeing it now so straight. 'I appreciate,' I said, 'the great decency of your not having hitherto spoken; but the time has certainly come to give me the whole thing.' She appeared to assent to this, but still only in silence; seeing which I went on: 'I must have it now. Of what did she die? Come, there was something between them.'

'There was everything.'

'In spite of the difference—?'

'Oh of their rank, their condition' – she brought it woefully out. '*She* was a lady.'

I turned it over; I again saw. 'Yes – she was a lady.'

'And he so dreadfully below,' said Mrs. Grose.

I felt that I doubtless needn't press too hard, in such company, on the place of a servant in the scale; but there was nothing to prevent an acceptance of my companion's own measure of my predecessor's abasement. There was a way to deal with that, and I dealt; the more readily for my full vision – on the evidence – of our employer's late clever good-looking 'own' man; impudent, assured, spoiled, depraved. 'The fellow was a hound.'

Mrs. Grose considered as if it were perhaps a little a case for a sense of shades. 'I've never seen one like him. He did what he wished.'

'With *her*?'

'With them all.'

It was as if now in my friend's own eyes Miss Jessel had again appeared. I seemed at any rate for an instant to trace their evocation of her as distinctly as I had seen her by the pond; and I brought out with decision: 'It must have been also what *she* wished!'

Mrs. Grose's face signified that it had been indeed, but she said at the same time: 'Poor woman – she paid for it!'

'Then you do know what she died of?' I asked.

'No – I know nothing. I wanted not to know; I was glad enough I didn't; and I thanked heaven she was well out of this!'

'Yet you had then your idea—'

'Of her real reason for leaving? Oh yes – as to that. She

couldn't have stayed. Fancy it here – for a governess! And afterwards I imagined – and I still imagine. And what I imagine is dreadful.'

'Not so dreadful as what *I* do,' I replied; on which I must have shown her – as I was indeed but too conscious – a front of miserable defeat. It brought out again all her compassion for me, and at the renewed touch of her kindness my power to resist broke down. I burst, as I had the other time made her burst, into tears; she took me to her motherly breast, where my lamentation overflowed. 'I don't do it!' I sobbed in despair; 'I don't save or shield them! It's far worse than I dreamed. They're lost!'

VIII

What I had said to Mrs. Grose was true enough: there were in the matter I had put before her depths and possibilities that I lacked resolution to sound; so that when we met once more in the wonder of it we were of a common mind about the duty of resistance to extravagant fancies. We were to keep our heads if we should keep nothing else – difficult indeed as that might be in the face of all that, in our prodigious experience, seemed least to be questioned. Late that night, while the house slept, we had another talk in my room; when she went all the way with me as to its being beyond doubt that I had seen exactly what I had seen. I found that to keep her thoroughly in the grip of this I had only to ask her how, if I had 'made it up', I came to be able to give, of each of the persons appearing to me, a picture disclosing, to the last detail, their special marks – a portrait on the exhibition of which she had instantly recognized and named them. She wished, of course – small blame to her! – to sink the whole subject; and I was quick to assure her that my own interest in it had now violently taken the form of a search for the way to escape from it. I closed with her cordially on the article of the likelihood that with recurrence – for recurrence we took for granted – I should get used to my danger; distinctly professing that my personal exposure had suddenly become the least of my discomforts. It was my new suspicion that was intolerable; and yet even to this complication the later hours of the day had brought a little ease.

On leaving her, after my first outbreak, I had of course returned to my pupils, associating the right remedy for my dismay with that sense of their charm which I had already recognized as a resource I could positively cultivate and which had never failed me yet. I had simply, in other words, plunged afresh into Flora's special society and there become aware – it was almost a luxury! – that she could put her little conscious hand straight upon the spot that ached. She had looked at me in sweet speculation and then had accused me to my face of having 'cried'. I had supposed the ugly signs of it brushed away; but I could literally – for the time at all events – rejoice, under this fathomless charity, that they had not entirely disappeared. To gaze into the depths of blue of the child's eyes and pronounce their loveliness a trick of premature cunning was to be guilty of a cynicism in preference to which I naturally preferred to abjure my judgement and, so far as might be, my agitation. I couldn't abjure for merely wanting to, but I could repeat to Mrs. Grose – as I did there, over and over, in the small hours – that with our small friends' voices in the air, their pressure on one's heart and their fragrant faces against one's cheek, everything fell to the ground but their incapacity and their beauty. It was a pity that, somehow, to settle this once for all, I had equally to re-enumerate the signs of subtlety that, in the afternoon, by the lake, had made a miracle of my show of self-possession. It was a pity to be obliged to re-investigate the certitude of the moment itself and repeat how it had come to me as a revelation that the inconceivable communion I then surprised must have been for both parties a matter of habit. It was a pity I should have had to quaver out again the reasons for my not having, in my delusion, so much as questioned that the little girl saw our visitant even as I actually saw Mrs. Grose herself, and that she wanted, by just so much as she did thus see, to make me suppose she didn't, and at the same time, without showing anything, arrive at a guess as to whether I myself did! It was a pity I needed to recapitulate the portentous little activities by which she sought to divert my attention – the perceptible increase of movement, the greater intensity of play, the singing, the gabbling of nonsense and the invitation to romp.

Yet if I had not indulged, to prove there was nothing in it, in this review, I should have missed the two or three dim elements of comfort that still remained to me. I shouldn't for instance have been able to asseverate to my friend that I was certain –

which was so much to the good – that *I* at least had not betrayed myself. I shouldn't have been prompted, by stress of need, by desperation of mind – I scarce know what to call it – to invoke such further aid to intelligence as might spring from pushing my colleague fairly to the wall. She had told me, bit by bit, under pressure, a great deal; but a small shifty spot on the wrong side of it all still sometimes brushed my brow like the wing of a bat; and I remember how on this occasion – for the sleeping house and the concentration alike of our danger and our watch seemed to help – I felt the importance of giving the last jerk to the curtain. 'I don't believe anything so horrible,' I recollect saying; 'no, let us put it definitely, my dear, that I don't. But if I did, you know, there's a thing I should require now, just without sparing you the least bit more – oh not a scrap, come! – to get out of you. What was it you had in mind when, in our distress, before Miles came back, over the letter from his school, you said, under my insistence, that you didn't pretend for him he hadn't literally *ever* been "bad"? He has *not*, truly, "ever," in these weeks that I myself have lived with him and so closely watched him; he has been an imperturbable little prodigy of delightful loveable goodness. Therefore you might perfectly have made the claim for him if you had not, as it happened, seen an exception to take. What was your exception, and to what passage in your personal observation of him did you refer?'

It was a straight question enough, but levity was not our note, and in any case I had before the grey dawn admonished us to separate got my answer. What my friend had had in mind proved immensely to the purpose. It was neither more nor less than the particular fact that for a period of several months Quint and the boy had been perpetually together. It was indeed the very appropriate item of evidence of her having ventured to criticize the propriety, to hint at the incongruity, of so close an alliance, and even to go so far on the subject as a frank overture to Miss Jessel would take her. Miss Jessel had, with a very high manner about it, requested her to mind her business, and the good woman had on this directly approached little Miles. What she had said to him, since I pressed, was that *she* liked to see young gentlemen not forget their station.

I pressed again, of course, the closer for that. 'You reminded him that Quint was only a base menial?'

'As you might say! And it was his answer, for one thing, that was bad.'

'And for another thing?' I waited. 'He repeated your words to Quint?'

'No, not that. It's just what he *wouldn't*!' she could still impress on me. 'I was sure, at any rate,' she added, 'that he didn't. But he denied certain occasions.'

'What occasions?'

'When they had been about together quite as if Quint were his tutor – and a very grand one – and Miss Jessel only for the little lady. When he had gone off with the fellow, I mean, and spent hours with him.'

'He then prevaricated about it – he said he hadn't?' Her assent was clear enough to cause me to add in a moment: 'I see. He lied.'

'Oh!' Mrs. Grose mumbled. This was a suggestion that it didn't matter; which indeed she backed up by a further remark. 'You see, after all, Miss Jessel didn't mind. She didn't forbid him.'

I considered. 'Did he put that to you as a justification?'

At this she dropped again. 'No, he never spoke of it.'

'Never mentioned her in connexion with Quint?'

She saw, visibly flushing, where I was coming out. 'Well, he didn't show anything. He denied,' she repeated; 'he denied.'

Lord, how I pressed her now! 'So that you could see he knew what was between the two wretches?'

'I don't know – I don't know!' the poor woman wailed.

'You do know, you dear thing,' I replied; 'only you haven't my dreadful boldness of mind, and you keep back, out of timidity and modesty and delicacy, even the impression that in the past, when you had, without my aid, to flounder about in silence, most of all made you miserable. But I shall get it out of you yet! There was something in the boy that suggested to you,' I continued, 'his covering and concealing their relation.'

'Oh he couldn't prevent—'

'Your learning the truth? I dare say! But, heavens,' I fell, with vehemence, a-thinking, 'what it shows that they must, to that extent, have succeeded in making of him!'

'Ah nothing that's not nice *now*!' Mrs. Grose lugubriously pleaded.

'I don't wonder you looked queer,' I persisted, 'when I mentioned to you the letter from his school!'

'I doubt if I looked as queer as you!' she retorted with homely force. 'And if he was so bad then as that comes to, how is he such an angel now?'

'Yes indeed – and if he was a fiend at school! How, how, how? Well,' I said in my torment, 'you must put it to me again, though I shall not be able to tell you for some days. Only put it to me again!' I cried in a way that made my friend stare. 'There are directions in which I mustn't for the present let myself go.' Meanwhile I returned to her first example – the one to which she had just previously referred – of the boy's happy capacity for an occasional slip. 'If Quint – on your remonstrance at the time you speak of – was a base menial, one of the things Miles said to you, I find myself guessing, was that you were another.' Again her admission was so adequate that I continued: 'And you forgave him that?'

'Wouldn't *you*?'

'Oh yes!' And we exchanged there, in the stillness, a sound of the oddest amusement. Then I went on: 'At all events, while he was with the man—'

'Miss Flora was with the woman. It suited them all!'

It suited me too, I felt, only too well; by which I mean that it suited exactly the particular deadly view I was in the very act of forbidding myself to entertain. But I so far succeeded in checking the expression of this view that I will throw, just here, no further light on it than may be offered by the mention of my final observation to Mrs. Grose. 'His having lied and been impudent are, I confess, less engaging specimens than I had hoped to have from you of the outbreak in him of the little natural man. Still,' I mused, 'they must do, for they make me feel more than ever that I must watch.'

It made me blush, the next minute, to see in my friend's face how much more unreservedly she had forgiven him than her anecdote struck me as pointing out to my own tenderness any way to do. This was marked when, at the schoolroom door, she quitted me. 'Surely you don't accuse *him*—'

'Of carrying on an intercourse that he conceals from me? Ah remember that, until further evidence, I now accuse nobody.' Then before shutting her out to go by another passage to her own place, 'I must just wait,' I wound up.

IX

I waited and waited, and the days took as they elapsed something from my consternation. A very few of them, in fact, passing, in constant sight of my pupils, without a fresh incident, sufficed to give to grievous fancies and even to odious memories a kind of brush of the sponge. I have spoken of the surrender to their extraordinary childish grace as a thing I could actively promote in myself, and it may be imagined if I neglected now to apply at this source for whatever balm it would yield. Stranger than I can express, certainly, was the effort to struggle against my new lights. It would doubtless have been a greater tension still, however, had it not been so frequently successful. I used to wonder how my little charges could help guessing that I thought strange things about them; and the circumstance that these things only made them more interesting was not by itself a direct aid to keeping them in the dark. I trembled lest they should see that they *were* so immensely more interesting. Putting things at the worst, at all events, as in meditation I so often did, any clouding of their innocence could only be – blameless and foredoomed as they were – a reason the more for taking risks. There were moments when I knew myself to catch them up by an irresistible impulse and press them to my heart. As soon as I had done so I used to wonder – 'What will they think of that? Doesn't it betray too much?' It would have been easy to get into a sad wild tangle about how much I might betray; but the real account, I feel, of the hours of peace I could still enjoy was that the immediate charm of my companions was a beguilement still effective even under the shadow of the possibility that it was studied. For if it occurred to me that I might occasionally excite suspicion by the little outbreaks of my sharper passion for them, so too I remember asking if I mightn't see a queerness in the traceable increase of their own demonstrations.

They were at this period extravagantly and preternaturally fond of me; which, after all, I could reflect, was no more than a graceful response in children perpetually bowed down over and hugged. The homage of which they were so lavish succeeded in truth for my nerves quite as well as if I never appeared to myself, as I may say, literally to catch them at a purpose in it. They had never, I think, wanted to do so many things for their poor protectress; I mean – though they got their lessons better and better, which was naturally what would please her most – in the way of diverting, entertaining, surprising her; reading her passages, telling her stories, acting her charades, pouncing out at her, in disguises, as animals and historical characters, and above all astonishing her by the 'pieces' they had secretly got by heart and could interminably recite. I should never get to the bottom – were I to let myself go even now – of the prodigious private commentary, all under still more private correction, with which I in these days overscored their full hours. They had shown me from the first a facility for everything, a general faculty which, taking a fresh start, achieved remarkable flights. They got their little tasks as if they loved them; they indulged, from the mere exuberance of the gift, in the most unimposed little miracles of memory. They not only popped out at me as tigers and as Romans, but as Shakespeareans, astronomers and navigators. This was so singularly the case that it had presumably much to do with the fact as to which, at the present day, I am at a loss for a different explanation: I allude to my unnatural composure on the subject of another school for Miles. What I remember is that I was content for the time not to open the question, and that contentment must have sprung from the sense of his perpetually striking show of cleverness. He was too clever for a bad governess, for a parson's daughter, to spoil; and the strangest if not the brightest thread in the pensive embroidery I just spoke of was the impression I might have got, if I had dared to work it out, that he was under some influence operating in his small intellectual life as a tremendous incitement.

If it was easy to reflect, however, that such a boy could postpone school, it was at least as marked that for such a boy to have been 'kicked out' by a school-master was a mystification without end. Let me add that in their company now – and I was careful almost never to be out of it – I could follow no scent very far. We lived in a cloud of music and affection and success and private theatricals. The musical sense in each of the children was of the quickest, but the elder in especial had a marvellous knack of catching and repeating. The schoolroom piano broke into all gruesome fancies; and when that failed there were confabulations in corners, with a sequel of one of them going out in the highest spirits in order to 'come in' as something new. I had had brothers myself, and it was no revelation to me that little girls could be slavish idolaters of little boys. What surpassed everything was that there was a little boy in the world who could have for the inferior age, sex and intelligence so fine a consideration. They were extraordinarily at one, and to say that they never either quarrelled or complained is to make the note of praise coarse for their quality of sweetness. Sometimes perhaps indeed (when I dropped into coarseness) I came across traces of little understandings between them by which one of them should keep me occupied while the other slipped away. There is a naïf side, I suppose, in all diplomacy; but if my pupils practised upon me it was surely with the minimum of grossness. It was all in the other quarter that, after a lull, the grossness broke out.

I find that I really hang back; but I must take my horrid plunge. In going on with the record of what was hideous at Bly I not only challenge the most liberal faith – for which I little care; but (and this is another matter) I renew what I myself suffered, I again push my dreadful way through it to the end.[1] There came suddenly an hour after which, as I look back, the business seems to me to have been all pure suffering; but I have at least reached the heart of it, and the straightest road out is doubtless to advance. One evening – with nothing to lead up or prepare it – I felt the cold touch of the impression that had breathed on me the night of my arrival and which, much lighter then as I have mentioned, I should probably have made little of in memory had my subsequent sojourn been less agitated. I had not gone to bed; I sat reading by a couple of candles. There was a roomful of old books at Bly – last-century fiction some of it, which, to the extent of a distinctly deprecated renown, but never to so much as that of a stray specimen, had reached the sequestered home and appealed to the unavowed curiosity of my youth. I remember that the book I had in my hand was Fielding's 'Amelia';[2] also that I was wholly awake. I recall further both a general conviction that it was horribly late and a particular objection to looking at my watch. I figure finally that the white curtain draping, in the fashion of those days, the head of Flora's little bed, shrouded, as I had assured myself long before, the perfection of childish rest. I recollect in short that though I was deeply interested in my author I found myself, at the turn of a page and with his spell all scattered, looking straight up from him and hard at the door of my room. There was a moment during which I listened, reminded of the faint sense I had had, the first night, of there being something undefinably astir in the house, and noted the soft breath of the open casement just move the half-drawn blind. Then, with all the marks of a deliberation that must have seemed magnificent had there been any one to admire it, I laid down my book, rose to my feet and, taking a candle, went straight out of the room and, from the passage, on which my light made little impression, noiselessly closed and locked the door.

I can say now neither what determined nor what guided me, but I went straight along the lobby, holding my candle high, till I came within sight of the tall window that presided over the great turn of the staircase. At this point I precipitately found myself aware of three things. They were practically simultaneous, yet they had flashes of succession. My candle, under a bold flourish, went out, and I perceived, by the uncovered window, that the yielding dusk of earliest morning rendered it unnecessary. Without it, the next instant, I knew that there was a figure on the stair. I speak of sequences, but I required no lapse of seconds to stiffen myself for a third encounter with Quint. The apparition had reached the landing halfway up and was therefore on the spot nearest the window, where, at sight of me, it stopped short and fixed me exactly as it had fixed me from the tower and from the garden. He knew me as well as I knew him; and so, in the cold faint twilight, with a glimmer in the high glass and another on the polish of the oak stair below, we faced each other in our common intensity. He was absolutely, on this occasion, a living detestable dangerous presence. But that was not the wonder of wonders; I reserve this distinction for quite another circumstance: the circumstance that dread had unmistakeably quitted me and that there was nothing in me unable to meet and measure him.

I had plenty of anguish after that extraordinary moment, but I had, thank God, no terror. And he knew I hadn't – I found myself at the end of an instant magnificently aware of this. I felt, in a fierce rigour of confidence, that if I stood my ground a minute I should cease – for the time at least – to have him to reckon with; and during the minute, accordingly, the thing was as human and hideous as a real interview: hideous just because it *was* human, as human as to have met alone, in the small hours, in a sleeping house, some enemy, some adventurer, some criminal. It was the dead silence of our long gaze at such close quarters that gave the whole horror, huge as it was, its only note of the unnatural. If I had met a murderer in such a place and at such an hour we still at least would have spoken. Something would have passed, in life, between us; if nothing had passed one of us would have moved. The moment was so prolonged that it would have taken but little more to make me doubt if even *I* were in life. I can't express what followed it save by saying that the silence itself – which was indeed in a manner an attestation of my strength – became the element into which I saw the figure disappear; in which I definitely saw it turn, as I might have seen the low wretch to which it had once belonged turn on receipt of an order, and pass, with my eyes on the villainous back that no hunch could have more disfigured, straight down the staircase and into the darkness in which the next bend was lost.

X

I remained a while at the top of the stair, but with the effect presently of understanding that when my visitor had gone, he had gone; then I returned to my room. The foremost thing I saw there by the light of the candle I had left burning was that Flora's little bed was empty; and on this I caught my breath with all the terror that, five minutes before, I had been able to resist. I dashed at the place in which I had left her lying and over which – for the small silk counterpane and the sheets were disarranged – the white curtains had been deceivingly pulled forward; then my step, to my unutterable relief, produced an answering sound: I noticed an agitation of the window-blind, and the child, ducking down, emerged rosily from the other side of it. She stood there in so much of her candour and so little of her night-gown, with her pink bare feet and the golden glow of her curls. She looked intensely grave, and I had never had such a sense of losing an advantage acquired (the thrill of which had just been so prodigious) as on my consciousness that she addressed me with a reproach – 'You naughty: where *have* you been?' Instead of challenging her own irregularity I found myself arraigned and explaining. She herself explained, for that matter, with the loveliest eagerest simplicity. She had known suddenly, as she lay there, that I was out of the room, and had jumped up to see what had become of me. I had dropped, with the joy of her reappearance, back into my chair – feeling then, and then only, a little faint; and she had pattered straight over to me, thrown herself upon my knee, given herself to be held with the flame of the candle full in the wonderful little face that was still flushed with sleep. I remember closing my eyes an instant, yieldingly, consciously, as before the excess of something beautiful that shone out of the blue of her own. 'You were looking for me out of the window?' I said. 'You thought I might be walking in the grounds?'

'Well, you know, I thought some one was' – she never blanched as she smiled out that at me.

Oh how I looked at her now! 'And did you see any one?'

'Ah *no*!' she returned almost (with the full privilege of childish inconsequence) resentfully, though with a long sweetness in her little drawl of the negative.

At that moment, in the state of my nerves, I absolutely believed she lied; and if I once more closed my eyes it was before the dazzle of the three or four possible ways in which I might take this up. One of these for a moment tempted me with such singular force that, to resist it, I must have gripped my little girl with a spasm that, wonderfully, she submitted to without a cry or a sign of fright. Why not break out at her on the spot and have it all over? – give it to her straight in her lovely little lighted face? 'You see, you see, you *know* that you do and that you already quite suspect I believe it; therefore why not frankly confess it to me, so that we may at least live with it together and learn perhaps, in the strangeness of our fate, where we are and what it means?' This solicitation dropped, alas, as it came: if I could immediately have succumbed to it I might have spared myself – well, you'll see what. Instead of succumbing I sprang again to my feet, looked at her bed and took a helpless middle way. 'Why did you pull the curtain over the place to make me think you were still there?'

Flora luminously considered; after which, with her little divine smile: 'Because I don't like to frighten you!'

'But if I had, by your idea, gone out—?'

She absolutely declined to be puzzled; she turned her eyes to the flame of the candle as if the question were as irrelevant, or at any rate as impersonal, as Mrs. Marcet[1] or nine-times-nine. 'Oh but you know,' she quite adequately answered, 'that you might come back, you dear, and that you *have*!' And after a little, when she had got into bed, I had, a long time, by almost sitting on her for the retention of her hand, to show how I recognized the pertinence of my return.

You may imagine the general complexion, from that moment, of my nights. I repeatedly sat up till I didn't know when; I selected moments when my room-mate unmistakeably slept, and, stealing out, took noiseless turns in the passage. I even pushed as far as to where I had last met Quint. But I never met him there again, and I may as well say at once that I on no other occasion saw him in the house. I just missed, on the staircase, nevertheless, a different adventure. Looking down it from the top I once recognized the presence of a woman seated on one of the lower steps with her back presented to me, her body half-bowed and her head, in an attitude of woe, in her hands. I had been there but an instant, however, when she vanished without looking round at me. I knew, for all that, exactly what dreadful face she had to show; and I wondered whether, if instead of being above I had been below, I should have had the same nerve for going up that I had lately shown Quint. Well, there continued to be plenty of call for nerve. On the eleventh night after my latest encounter with that gentleman – they were all numbered now – I had an alarm that perilously skirted it and that indeed, from the particular quality of its unexpectedness, proved quite my sharpest shock. It was precisely the first night during this series that, weary with vigils, I had conceived I might again without laxity lay myself down at my old hour. I slept immediately and, as I afterwards knew, till about one o'clock; but when I woke it was to sit straight up, as completely roused as if a hand had shaken me. I had left a light burning, but it was now out, and I felt an instant certainty that Flora had extinguished it. This brought me to my feet and straight, in the darkness, to her bed, which I found she had left. A glance at the window enlightened me further, and the striking of a match completed the picture.

The child had again got up – this time blowing out the taper, and had again, for some purpose of observation or response, squeezed in behind the blind and was peering out into the night. That she now saw – as she had not, I had satisfied myself, the previous time – was proved to me by the fact that she was disturbed neither by my re-illumination nor by the haste I made to get into slippers and into a wrap. Hidden, protected, absorbed, she evidently rested on the sill – the casement opened forward

– and gave herself up. There was a great still moon to help her, and this fact had counted in my quick decision. She was face to face with the apparition we had met at the lake, and could now communicate with it as she had not then been able to do. What I, on my side, had to care for was, without disturbing her, to reach, from the corridor, some other window turned to the same quarter. I got to the door without her hearing me; I got out of it, closed it and listened, from the other side, for some sound from her. While I stood in the passage I had my eyes on her brother's door, which was but ten steps off and which, indescribably, produced in me a renewal of the strange impulse that I lately spoke of as my temptation. What if I should go straight in and march to *his* window? – what if, by risking to his boyish bewilderment a revelation of my motive, I should throw across the rest of the mystery the long halter of my boldness?

This thought held me sufficiently to make me cross to his threshold and pause again. I preternaturally listened; I figured to myself what might portentously be; I wondered if his bed were also empty and he also secretly at watch. It was a deep soundless minute, at the end of which my impulse failed. He was quiet; he might be innocent; the risk was hideous; I turned away. There was a figure in the grounds – a figure prowling for a sight, the visitor with whom Flora was engaged; but it wasn't the visitor most concerned with my boy. I hesitated afresh, but on other grounds and only a few seconds; then I had made my choice. There were empty rooms enough at Bly, and it was only a question of choosing the right one. The right one suddenly presented itself to me as the lower one – though high above the gardens – in the solid corner of the house that I have spoken of as the old tower. This was a large square chamber, arranged with some state as a bedroom, the extravagant size of which made it so inconvenient that it had not for years, though kept by Mrs. Grose in exemplary order, been occupied. I had often admired it and I knew my way about in it; I had only, after just faltering at the first chill gloom of its disuse, to pass across it and unbolt in all quietness one of the shutters. Achieving this transit I uncovered the glass without a sound and, applying my face to the pane, was able, the darkness without being much less than within, to see that I commanded the right direction. Then I saw something more. The moon made the night extraordinarily penetrable and showed me on the lawn a person, diminished by distance, who stood there motionless and as if fascinated, looking up to where I had appeared – looking, that is, not so much straight at me as at something that was apparently above me. There was clearly another person above me – there was a person on the tower; but the presence on the lawn was not in the least what I had conceived and had confidently hurried to meet. The presence on the lawn – I felt sick as I made it out – was poor little Miles himself.

XI

It was not till late next day that I spoke to Mrs. Grose; the rigour with which I kept my pupils in sight making it often difficult to meet her privately: the more as we each felt the importance of not provoking – on the part of the servants quite as much as on that of the children – any suspicion of a secret flurry or of a discussion of mysteries. I drew a great security in this particular from her mere smooth aspect. There was nothing in her fresh face to pass on to others the least of my horrible confidences. She believed me, I was sure, absolutely: if she hadn't I don't know what would have become of me, for I couldn't have borne the strain alone. But she was a magnificent monument to the blessing of a want of imagination, and if she could see in our little charges nothing but their beauty and amiability, their happiness and cleverness, she had no direct communication with the sources of my trouble. If they had been at all visibly blighted or battered she would doubtless have grown, on tracing it back, haggard enough to match them; as matters stood, however, I could feel her, when she surveyed them with her large white arms folded and the habit of serenity in all her look, thank the Lord's mercy that if they were ruined the pieces would still serve. Flights of fancy gave place, in her mind, to a steady fireside glow, and I had already begun to perceive how, with the development of the conviction that – as time went on without a public accident – our young things could, after all, look out for themselves, she addressed her greatest solicitude to the sad case presented by their deputy-guardian. That, for myself, was a sound simplification: I could engage that, to the world, my face should tell no tales, but it would have been, in the conditions, an immense added worry to find myself anxious about hers.

At the hour I now speak of she had joined me, under pressure, on the terrace, where, with the lapse of the season, the afternoon sun was now agreeable; and we sat there together while before us and at a distance, yet within call if we wished, the children strolled to and fro in one of their most manageable moods. They moved slowly, in unison, below us, over the lawn, the boy, as they went, reading aloud from a story-book and passing his arm round his sister to keep her quite in touch. Mrs. Grose watched them with positive placidity; then I caught the suppressed intellectual creak with which she conscientiously turned to take from me a view of the back of the tapestry. I had made her a receptacle of lurid things, but there was an odd recognition of my superiority – my accomplishments and my function – in her patience under my pain. She offered her mind to my disclosures as, had I wished to mix a witch's broth and proposed it with assurance, she would have held out a large clean saucepan. This had become thoroughly her attitude by the time that, in my recital of the events of the night, I reached the point of what Miles had said to me when, after seeing him, at such a monstrous hour, almost on the very spot where he happened now to be, I had gone down to bring him in; choosing then, at the window, with a concentrated need of not alarming the house, rather that method than any noisier process. I had left her meanwhile in little doubt of my small hope of representing with success even to her actual sympathy my sense of the real splendour of the little inspiration with which, after I had got him into the house, the boy met my final articulate challenge. As soon as I appeared in the moonlight on the terrace he had come to me as straight as possible; on which I had taken his hand without a word and led him, through the dark spaces, up the staircase where Quint had so hungrily hovered for him, along the lobby where I had listened and trembled, and so to his forsaken room.

Not a sound, on the way, had passed between us, and I had wondered – oh *how* I had wondered! – if he were groping about in his dreadful little mind for something plausible and not too grotesque. It would tax his invention certainly, and I felt, this time, over his real embarrassment, a curious thrill of triumph. It was a sharp trap for any game hitherto successful. He could play no longer at perfect propriety, nor could he pretend to it; so how the deuce would he get out of the scrape? There beat in me indeed, with the passionate throb of this question, an equal dumb appeal as to how the deuce *I* should. I was confronted at last, as never yet, with all the risk attached even now to sounding my own horrid note. I remember in fact that as we pushed into his little chamber, where the bed had not been slept in at all and the window, uncovered to the moonlight, made the place so clear that there was no need of striking a match – I remember how I suddenly dropped, sank upon the edge of the bed from the force of the idea that he must know how he really, as they say, 'had' me. He could do what he liked, with all his cleverness to help him, so long as I should continue to defer to the old tradition of the criminality of those caretakers of the young who minister to superstitions and fears. He 'had' me indeed, and in a cleft stick; for who would ever absolve me, who would consent that I should go unhung, if, by the faintest tremor of an overture, I were the first to introduce into our perfect intercourse an element so dire? No, no: it was useless to attempt to convey to Mrs. Grose, just as it is scarcely less so to attempt to suggest here, how, during our short stiff brush there in the dark, he fairly shook me with admiration. I was of course thoroughly kind and merciful; never, never yet had I placed on his small shoulders hands of such tenderness as those with which, while I rested against the bed, I held him there well under fire. I had no alternative but, in form at least, to put it to him.

'You must tell me now – and all the truth. What did you go out for? What were you doing there?'

I can still see his wonderful smile, the whites of his beautiful eyes and the uncovering of his clear teeth, shine to me in the dusk. 'If I tell you why, will you understand?' My heart, at this, leaped into my mouth. *Would* he tell me why? I found no sound on my lips to press it, and I was aware of answering only with a vague repeated grimacing nod. He was gentleness itself, and while I wagged my head at him he stood there more than ever a little fairy prince. It was his brightness indeed that gave me a respite. Would it be so great if he were really going to tell me? 'Well,' he said at last, 'just exactly in order that you should do this.'

'Do what?'

'Think me – for a change – *bad*!' I shall never forget the sweetness and gaiety with which he brought out the word, nor how, on top of it, he bent forward and kissed me. It was practically the end of everything. I met his kiss and I had to make, while I folded him for a minute in my arms, the most stupendous effort not to cry. He had given exactly the account of himself that permitted least my going behind it, and it was only with the effect of confirming my acceptance of it that, as I presently glanced about the room, I could say—

'Then you didn't undress at all?'

He fairly glittered in the gloom. 'Not at all. I sat up and read.'

'And when did you go down?'

'At midnight. When I'm bad I *am* bad!'

'I see, I see – it's charming. But how could you be sure I should know it?'

'Oh I arranged that with Flora.' His answers rang out with a readiness! 'She was to get up and look out.'

'Which is what she did do.' It was I who fell into the trap!

'So she disturbed you, and, to see what she was looking at, you also looked – you saw.'

'While you,' I concurred, 'caught your death in the night air!'

He literally bloomed so from this exploit that he could afford radiantly to assent. 'How otherwise should I have been bad enough?' he asked. Then, after another embrace, the incident and our interview closed on my recognition of all the reserves of goodness that, for his joke, he had been able to draw upon.

XII

The particular impression I had received proved in the morning light, I repeat, not quite successfully presentable to Mrs. Grose, though I re-enforced it with the mention of still another remark that he had made before we separated. 'It all lies in half a dozen words,' I said to her, 'words that really settle the matter. "Think, you know, what I *might* do!" He threw that off to show me how good he is. He knows down to the ground what he "might do". That's what he gave them a taste of at school.'

'Lord, you do change!' cried my friend.

'I don't change – I simply make it out. The four, depend upon it, perpetually meet. If on either of these last nights you had been with either child you'd clearly have understood. The more I've watched and waited the more I've felt that if there were nothing else to make it sure it would be made so by the systematic silence of each. *Never*, by a slip of the tongue, have they so much as alluded to either of their old friends, any more than Miles has alluded to his expulsion. Oh yes, we may sit here and look at them, and they may show off to us there to their fill; but even while they pretend to be lost in their fairy-tale they're steeped in their vision of the dead restored to them. He's not reading to her,' I declared; 'they're talking of *them* – they're talking horrors! I go on, I know, as if I were crazy; and it's a wonder I'm not. What I've seen would have made *you* so; but it has only made me more lucid, made me get hold of still other things.'

My lucidity must have seemed awful, but the charming creatures who were victims of it, passing and repassing in their interlocked sweetness, gave my colleague something to hold on by; and I felt how tight she held as, without stirring in the breath of my passion, she covered them still with her eyes. 'Of what other things have you got hold?'

'Why of the very things that have delighted, fascinated and yet, at bottom, as I now so strangely see, mystified and troubled me. Their more than earthly beauty, their absolutely unnatural goodness. It's a game,' I went on; 'it's a policy and a fraud!'

'On the part of little darlings—?'

'As yet mere lovely babies? Yes, mad as that seems!' The very act of bringing it out really helped me to trace it – follow it all up and piece it all together. 'They haven't been good – they've only been absent. It has been easy to live with them because they're simply leading a life of their own. They're not mine – they're not ours. They're his and they're hers!'

'Quint's and that woman's?'

'Quint's and that woman's. They want to get to them.'

Oh how, at this, poor Mrs. Grose appeared to study them! 'But for what?'

'For the love of all the evil that, in those dreadful days, the pair put into them. And to ply them with that evil still, to keep up the work of demons, is what brings the others back.'

'Laws!' said my friend under her breath. The exclamation was homely, but it revealed a real acceptance of my further proof of what, in the bad time – for there had been a worse even than this! – must have occurred. There could have been no such justification for me as the plain assent of her experience to whatever depth of depravity I found credible in our brace of scoundrels. It was in obvious submission of memory that she brought out after a moment: 'They *were* rascals! But what can they now do?' she pursued.

'Do?' I echoed so loud that Miles and Flora, as they passed at their distance, paused an instant in their walk and looked at us. 'Don't they do enough?' I demanded in a lower tone, while the children, having smiled and nodded and kissed hands to us, resumed their exhibition. We were held by it a minute; then I answered: 'They can destroy them!' At this my companion did turn, but the appeal she launched was a silent one, the effect of which was to make me more explicit. 'They don't know as yet quite how – but they're trying hard. They're seen only across, as it were, and beyond – in strange places and on high places, the top of towers, the roof of houses, the outside of windows, the further edge of pools; but there's a deep design, on either side, to shorten the distance and overcome the obstacle: so the success of the tempters is only a question of time. They've only to keep to their suggestions of danger.'

'For the children to come?'

'And perish in the attempt!' Mrs. Grose slowly got up, and I scrupulously added: 'Unless, of course, we can prevent!'

Standing there before me while I kept my seat she visibly turned things over. 'Their uncle must do the preventing. He must take them away.'

'And who's to make him?'

She had been scanning the distance, but she now dropped on me a foolish face. 'You, Miss.'

'By writing to him that his house is poisoned and his little nephew and niece mad?'[1]

'But if they *are*, Miss?'

'And if I am myself, you mean? That's charming news to be sent him by a person enjoying his confidence and whose prime undertaking was to give him no worry.'

Mrs. Grose considered, following the children again. 'Yes, he do hate worry. That was the great reason—'

'Why those fiends took him in so long? No doubt, though his indifference must have been awful. As I'm not a fiend, at any rate, I shouldn't take him in.'

My companion, after an instant and for all answer, sat down again and grasped my arm. 'Make him at any rate come to you.'

I stared. 'To *me*?' I had a sudden fear of what she might do. '"Him"?'

'He ought to *be* here – he ought to help.'

I quickly rose and I think I must have shown her a queerer face than ever yet. 'You see me asking him for a visit?' No, with her eyes on my face she evidently couldn't. Instead of it even – as a woman reads another – she could see what I myself saw: his derision, his amusement, his contempt for the breakdown of my resignation at being left alone and for the fine machinery I had set in motion to attract his attention to my slighted charms. She didn't know – no one knew – how proud I had been to serve him and to stick to our terms; yet she none the less took the measure, I think, of the warning I now gave her. 'If you should so lose your head as to appeal to him for me—'

She was really frightened. 'Yes, Miss?'

'I would leave, on the spot, both him and you.'

XIII

It was all very well to join them, but speaking to them proved quite as much as ever an effort beyond my strength – offered, in close quarters, difficulties as insurmountable as before. This situation continued a month, and with new aggravations and particular notes, the note above all, sharper and sharper, of the small ironic consciousness on the part of my pupils. It was not, I am as sure to-day as I was sure then, my mere infernal imagination: it was absolutely traceable that they were aware of my predicament and that this strange relation made, in a manner, for a long time, the air in which we moved. I don't mean that they had their tongues in their cheeks or did anything vulgar, for that was not one of their dangers: I do mean, on the other hand, that the element of the unnamed and untouched became, between us, greater than any other, and that so much avoidance couldn't have been made successful without a great deal of tacit arrangement. It was as if, at moments, we were perpetually coming into sight of subjects before which we must stop short, turning suddenly out of alleys that we perceived to be blind, closing with a little bang that made us look at each other – for, like all bangs, it was something louder than we had intended – the doors we had indiscreetly opened. All roads lead to Rome, and there were times when it might have struck us that almost every branch of study or subject of conversation skirted forbidden ground. Forbidden ground was the question of the return of the dead in general and of whatever, in especial, might survive, for memory, of the friends little children had lost. There were days when I could have sworn that one of them had, with a small invisible nudge, said to the other: 'She thinks she'll do it this time

– but she *won't*!' To 'do it' would have been to indulge for instance – and for once in a way – in some direct reference to the lady who had prepared them for my discipline. They had a delightful endless appetite for passages in my own history to which I had again and again treated them; they were in possession of everything that had ever happened to me, had had, with every circumstance, the story of my smallest adventures and of those of my brothers and sisters and of the cat and the dog at home, as well as many particulars of the whimsical bent of my father, of the furniture and arrangement of our house and of the conversation of the old women of our village. There were things enough, taking one with another, to chatter about, if one went very fast and knew by instinct when to go round. They pulled with an art of their own the strings of my invention and my memory; and nothing else perhaps, when I thought of such occasions afterwards, gave me so the suspicion of being watched from under cover. It was in any case over *my* life, *my* past and *my* friends alone that we could take anything like our ease; a state of affairs that led them sometimes without the least pertinence to break out into sociable reminders. I was invited – with no visible connexion – to repeat afresh Goody Gosling's celebrated *mot* [1] or to confirm the details already supplied as to the cleverness of the vicarage pony.

It was partly at such junctures as these and partly at quite different ones that, with the turn my matters had now taken, my predicament, as I have called it, grew most sensible. The fact that the days passed for me without another encounter ought, it would have appeared, to have done something toward soothing my nerves. Since the light brush, that second night on the upper landing, of the presence of a woman at the foot of the stair, I had seen nothing, whether in or out of the house, that one had better not have seen. There was many a corner round which I expected to come upon Quint, and many a situation that, in a merely sinister way, would have favoured the appearance of Miss Jessel. The summer had turned, the summer had gone; the autumn had dropped upon Bly and had blown out half our lights. The place, with its grey sky and withered garlands, its bared spaces and scattered dead leaves, was like a theatre after the performance – all strewn with crumpled playbills. There were exactly states of the air, conditions of sound and of stillness, unspeakable impressions of the *kind* of ministering moment, that brought back to me, long enough to catch it, the feeling of the medium in which, that June evening out of doors, I had had my first sight of Quint, and in which too, at those other instants, I had, after seeing him through the window, looked for him in vain in the circle of shrubbery. I recognized the signs, the portents – I recognized the moment, the spot. But they remained unaccompanied and empty, and I continued unmolested; if unmolested one could call a young woman whose sensibility had, in the most extraordinary fashion, not declined but deepened. I had said in my talk with Mrs. Grose on that horrid scene of Flora's by the lake – and had perplexed her by so saying – that it would from that moment distress me much more to lose my power than to keep it. I had then expressed what was vividly in my mind: the truth that, whether the children really saw or not – since, that is, it was not yet definitely proved – I greatly preferred, as a safeguard, the fulness of my own exposure. I was ready to know the very worst that was to be known. What I had then had an ugly glimpse of was that my eyes might be sealed just while theirs were most opened. Well, my eyes *were* sealed, it appeared, at present – a consummation for which it seemed blasphemous not to thank God. There was, alas, a difficulty about that: I would have thanked him with all my soul had I not had in a proportionate measure this conviction of the secret of my pupils.

How can I retrace to-day the strange steps of my obsession? There were times of our being together when I would have been ready to swear that, literally, in my presence, but with my direct sense of it closed, they had visitors who were known and were welcome. Then it was that, had I not been deterred by the very chance that such an injury might prove greater than the injury to be averted, my exaltation would have broken out. 'They're here, they're here, you little wretches,' I would have cried, 'and you can't deny it now!' The little wretches denied it with all the added volume of their sociability and their tenderness, just in the crystal depths of which – like the flash of a fish in a stream – the mockery of their advantage peeped up. The shock had in truth sunk into me still deeper than I knew on the night when, looking out either for Quint or for Miss Jessel under the stars, I had seen there the boy over whose rest I watched and who had immediately brought in with him – had straightway there turned on me – the lovely upward look with which, from the battlements above us, the hideous apparition of Quint had played. If it was a question of a scare my discovery on this occasion had scared me more than any other, and it was essentially in the scared state that I drew my actual conclusions.[2] They harassed me so that sometimes, at odd moments, I shut myself up audibly to rehearse – it was at once a fantastic relief and a renewed despair – the manner in which I might come to the point. I approached it from one side and the other while, in my room, I flung myself about, but I always broke down in the monstrous utterance of names. As they died away on my lips I said to myself that I should indeed help them to represent something infamous if by pronouncing them I should violate as rare a little case of instinctive delicacy as any schoolroom probably had ever known. When I said to myself: '*They* have the manners to be silent, and you, trusted as you are, the baseness to speak!' I felt myself crimson and covered my face with my hands. After these secret scenes I chattered more than ever, going on volubly enough till one of our prodigious palpable hushes occurred – I can call them nothing else – the strange dizzy lift or swim (I try for terms!) into a stillness, a pause of all life, that had nothing to do with the more or less noise we at the moment might be engaged in making and that I could hear through any intensified mirth or quickened recitation or louder strum of the piano. Then it was that the others, the outsiders, were there. Though they were not angels they 'passed', as the French say, causing me, while they stayed, to tremble with the fear of their addressing to their younger victims some yet more infernal message or more vivid image than they had thought good enough for myself.

What it was least possible to get rid of was the cruel idea that, whatever I had seen, Miles and Flora saw *more* – things terrible and unguessable and that sprang from dreadful passages of intercourse in the past. Such things naturally left on the surface, for the time, a chill that we vociferously denied we felt; and we had all three, with repetition, got into such splendid training that we went, each time, to mark the close of the incident, almost automatically through the very same movements. It was striking of the children at all events to kiss me inveterately with a wild irrelevance and never to fail – one or the other – of the precious question that had helped us through many a peril. 'When do you think he *will* come? Don't you think we *ought* to write?' – there was nothing like that enquiry, we found by experience, for carrying off an awkwardness. 'He' of course was their uncle in Harley Street; and we lived in much profusion of theory that he might at any moment arrive to mingle in our circle. It was impossible to have given less encouragement than he had administered to such a doctrine, but if we had not had the doctrine to fall back upon we should have deprived each other of some of our finest exhibitions. He never wrote to them – that may have been selfish, but it was a part of the flattery of his trust of myself; for the way in which a man pays his highest tribute to a woman is apt to be but by the more festal celebration of one of the sacred laws of his comfort. So I held that I carried out the spirit of the pledge given not to appeal to him when I let our young friends understand that their own letters were but charming literary exercises. They were too beautiful to be posted; I kept them myself; I have them all to this hour. This was a rule indeed which only added to the satiric effect of my being plied with the supposition that he might at any moment be among us. It was exactly as if our young friends knew how almost more awkward than anything else that might be for me. There appears to me moreover as I look back no note in all this more extraordinary than the mere fact that, in spite of my tension and of their triumph, I never lost patience with them. Adorable they must in truth have been, I now feel, since I didn't in these days hate them! Would exasperation, however, if relief had longer been postponed, finally have betrayed me? It little matters, for relief arrived. I call it relief though it was only the relief that a snap brings to a strain or the burst of a thunderstorm to a day of suffocation. It was at least change, and it came with a rush.

XIV

Walking to church a certain Sunday morning, I had little Miles at my side and his sister, in advance of us and at Mrs. Grose's, well in sight. It was a crisp clear day, the first of its order for some time; the night had brought a touch of frost and thc autumn air, bright and sharp, made the church-bells almost gay. It was an odd accident of thought that I should have happened at such a moment to be particularly and very gratefully struck with the obedience of my little charges. Why did they never resent my inexorable, my perpetual society? Something or other had brought nearer home to me that I had all but pinned the boy to my shawl, and that in the way our companions were marshalled before me I might have appeared to provide against some danger of rebellion. I was like a gaoler with an eye to possible surprises and escapes. But all this belonged – I mean their magnificent little surrender – just to the special array of the facts that were most abysmal. Turned out for Sunday by his uncle's tailor, who had had a free hand and a notion of pretty waistcoats and of his grand little air, Miles's whole title to independence, the rights of his sex and situation, were so stamped upon him that if he had suddenly struck for freedom I should have had nothing to say. I was by the strangest of chances wondering how I should meet him when the revolution unmistakeably occurred. I call it a revolution because I now see how, with the word he spoke, the curtain rose on the last act of my dreadful drama and the catastrophe was precipitated. 'Look here, my dear, you know,' he charmingly said, 'when in the world, please, am I going back to school?'

Transcribed here the speech sounds harmless enough, particularly as uttered in the sweet, high, casual pipe with which, at all interlocutors, but above all at his eternal governess, he threw off intonations as if he were tossing roses. There was something in them that always made one 'catch', and I caught at any rate now so effectually that I stopped as short as if one of the trees of the park had fallen across the road. There was something new, on the spot, between us, and he was perfectly aware I recognized it, though to enable me to do so he had no need to look a whit less candid and charming than usual. I could feel in him how he already, from my at first finding nothing to reply, perceived the advantage he had gained. I was so slow to find anything that he had plenty of time, after a minute, to continue with his suggestive but inconclusive smile: 'You know, my dear, that for a fellow to be with a lady *always*—!' His 'my dear' was constantly on his lips for me, and nothing could have expressed more the exact shade of the sentiment with which I desired to inspire my pupils than its fond familiarity. It was so respectfully easy.

But oh how I felt that at present I must pick my own phrases! I remember that, to gain time, I tried to laugh, and I seemed to see in the beautiful face with which he watched me how ugly and queer I looked. 'And always with the same lady?' I returned.

He neither blenched nor winked. The whole thing was virtually out between us. 'Ah of course she's a jolly "perfect" lady; but after all I'm a fellow, don't you see? who's – well, getting on.'

I lingered there with him an instant ever so kindly.

'Yes, you're getting on.' Oh but I felt helpless! I have kept to this day the heartbreaking little idea of how he seemed to know that and to play with it. 'And you can't say I've not been awfully good, can you?'

I laid my hand on his shoulder, for though I felt how much better it would have been to walk on I was not yet quite able. 'No, I can't say that, Miles.'

'Except just that one night, you know—!'

'That one night?' I couldn't look as straight as he.

'Why when I went down – went out of the house.'

'Oh yes. But I forget what you did it for.'

'You forget?' – he spoke with the sweet extravagance of childish reproach. 'Why it was just to show you I could!'

'Oh yes – you could.'

'And I can again.'

I felt I might perhaps after all succeed in keeping my wits about me. 'Certainly. But you won't.'

'No, not *that* again. It was nothing.'

'It was nothing,' I said. 'But we must go on.'

He resumed our walk with me, passing his hand into my arm. 'Then when *am* I going back?'

I wore, in turning it over, my most responsible air. 'Were you very happy at school?'

He just considered. 'Oh I'm happy enough anywhere!'

'Well then,' I quavered, 'if you're just as happy here—!'

'Ah but that isn't everything! Of course *you* know a lot—'

'But you hint that you know almost as much?' I risked as he paused.

'Not half I want to!' Miles honestly professed. 'But it isn't so much that.'

'What is it then?'

'Well – I want to see more life.'

'I see; I see.' We had arrived within sight of the church and of various persons, including several of the household of Bly, on their way to it and clustered about the door to see us go in. I quickened our step; I wanted to get there before the question between us opened up much further; I reflected hungrily that he would have for more than an hour to be silent; and I thought with envy of the comparative dusk of the pew and of the almost spiritual help of the hassock on which I might bend my knees. I seemed literally to be running a race with some confusion to which he was about to reduce me, but I felt he had got in first when, before we had even entered the churchyard, he threw out—

'I want my own sort!'

It literally made me bound forward. 'There aren't many of your own sort, Miles!' I laughed. 'Unless perhaps dear little Flora!'

'You really compare me to a baby girl?'

This found me singularly weak. 'Don't you then *love* our sweet Flora?'

'If I didn't – and you too; if I didn't—!' he repeated as if retreating for a jump, yet leaving his thought so unfinished that, after we had come into the gate, another stop, which he imposed on me by the pressure of his arm, had become inevitable. Mrs. Grose and Flora had passed into the church, the other worshippers had followed and we were, for the minute, alone among the old thick graves. We had paused, on the path from the gate, by a low oblong table-like tomb.

'Yes, if you didn't—?'

He looked, while I waited, about at the graves. 'Well, you know what!' But he didn't move, and he presently produced something that made me drop straight down on the stone slab as if suddenly to rest. 'Does my uncle think what *you* think?'

I markedly rested. 'How do you know what I think?'

'Ah well, of course I don't; for it strikes me you never tell me. But I mean does *he* know?'

'Know what, Miles?'

'Why the way I'm going on.'

I recognized quickly enough that I could make, to this enquiry, no answer that wouldn't involve something of a sacrifice of my employer. Yet it struck me that we were all, at Bly, sufficiently sacrificed to make that venial. 'I don't think your uncle much cares.'

Miles, on this, stood looking at me. 'Then don't you think he can be made to?'

'In what way?'

'Why by his coming down.'

'But who'll get him to come down?'

'*I* will!' the boy said with extraordinary brightness and emphasis. He gave me another look charged with that expression and then marched off alone into church.

XV

The business was practically settled from the moment I never followed him. It was a pitiful surrender to agitation, but my being aware of this had somehow no power to restore me. I only sat there on my tomb and read into what our young friend had said to me the fulness of its meaning; by the time I had grasped the whole of which I had also embraced, for absence, the pretext that I was ashamed to offer my pupils and the rest of the congregation such an example of delay. What I said to myself above all was that Miles had got something out of me and that the gage of it for him would be just this awkward collapse. He had got out of me that there was something I was much afraid of, and that he should probably be able to make use of my fear to gain, for his own purpose, more freedom. My fear was of having to deal with the intolerable question of the grounds of his dismissal from school, since that was really but the question of the horrors gathered behind. That his uncle should arrive to treat with me of these things was a solution that, strictly speaking, I ought now to have desired to bring on; but I could so little face the ugliness and the pain of it that I simply procrastinated and lived from hand to mouth. The boy, to my deep discomposure, was immensely in the right, was in a position to say to me: 'Either you clear up with my guardian the mystery of this interruption of my studies, or you cease to expect me to lead with you a life that's so unnatural for a boy.' What was so unnatural for the particular boy I was concerned with was this sudden revelation of a consciousness and a plan.

That was what really overcame me, what prevented my going in. I walked round the church, hesitating, hovering; I reflected that I had already, with him, hurt myself beyond repair. Therefore I could patch up nothing and it was too extreme an effort to squeeze beside him into the pew: he would be so much more sure than ever to pass his arm into mine and make me sit there for an hour in close mute contact with his commentary on our talk. For the first minute since his arrival I wanted to get away from him. As I paused beneath the high east window and listened to the sounds of worship I was taken with an impulse that might master me, I felt, and completely, should I give it the least encouragement. I might easily put an end to my ordeal by getting away altogether. Here was my chance; there was no one to stop me; I could give the whole thing up – turn my back and bolt. It was only a question of hurrying again, for a few preparations, to the house which the attendance at church of so many of the servants would practically have left unoccupied. No one, in short, could blame me if I should just drive desperately off. What was it to get away if I should get away only till dinner? That would be in a couple of hours, at the end of which – I had the acute prevision – my little pupils would play at innocent wonder about my non-appearance in their train.

'What *did* you do, you naughty bad thing? Why in the world, to worry us so – and take our thoughts off too, don't you know? – did you desert us at the very door?' I couldn't meet such questions nor, as they asked them, their false little lovely eyes; yet it was all so exactly what I should have to meet that, as the prospect grew sharp to me, I at last let myself go.

I got, so far as the immediate moment was concerned, away; I came straight out of the churchyard and, thinking hard, retraced my steps through the park. It seemed to me that by the time I reached the house I had made up my mind to cynical flight. The Sunday stillness both of the approaches and of the interior, in which I met no one, fairly stirred me with a sense of opportunity. Were I to get off quickly this way I should get off without a scene, without a word. My quickness would have to be remarkable, however, and the question of a conveyance was the great one to settle. Tormented, in the hall, with difficulties and obstacles, I remember sinking down at the foot of the staircase – suddenly collapsing there on the lowest step and then, with a revulsion, recalling that it was exactly where, more than a month before, in the darkness of night and just so bowed with evil things, I had seen the spectre of the most horrible of women. At this I was able to straighten myself; I went the rest of the way up; I made, in my turmoil, for the schoolroom, where there were objects belonging to me that I should have to take. But I opened the door to find again, in a flash, my eyes unsealed. In the presence of what I saw I reeled straight back upon resistance.

Seated at my own table in the clear noonday light I saw a person whom, without my previous experience, I should have taken at the first blush for some house-maid who might have stayed at home to look after the place and who, availing herself of rare relief from observation and of the schoolroom table and my pens, ink and paper, had applied herself to the considerable effort of a letter to her sweetheart. There was an effort in the way that, while her arms rested on the table, her hands, with evident weariness, supported her head; but at the moment I took this in I had already become aware that, in spite of my entrance, her attitude strangely persisted. Then it was – with the very act of its announcing itself – that her identity flared up in a change of posture. She rose, not as if she had heard me, but with an indescribable grand melancholy of indifference and detachment, and, within a dozen feet of me, stood there as my vile predecessor. Dishonoured and tragic, she was all before me; but even as I fixed and, for memory, secured it, the awful image passed away. Dark as midnight in her black dress, her haggard beauty and her unutterable woe, she had looked at me long enough to appear to say that her right to sit at my table was as good as mine to sit at hers. While these instants lasted indeed I had the extraordinary chill of a feeling that it was I who was the intruder. It was as a wild protest against it that, actually addressing her – 'You terrible miserable woman!' – I heard myself break into a sound that, by the open door, rang through the long passage and the empty house. She looked at me as if she heard me, but I had recovered myself and cleared the air. There was nothing in the room the next minute but the sunshine and the sense that I must stay.

XVI

I had so perfectly expected the return of the others to be marked by a demonstration that I was freshly upset at having to find them merely dumb and discreet about my desertion. Instead of gaily denouncing and caressing me they made no allusion to my having failed them, and I was left, for the time, on perceiving that she too said nothing, to study Mrs. Grose's odd face. I did this to such purpose that I made sure they had in some way bribed her to silence; a silence that, however, I would engage to break down on the first private opportunity. This opportunity came before tea: I secured five minutes with her in the housekeeper's room, where, in the twilight, amid a smell of lately-baked bread, but with the place all swept and garnished, I found her sitting in pained placidity before the fire. So I see her still, so I see her best: facing the flame from her straight chair in the dusky shining room, a large clean picture of the 'put away' – of drawers closed and locked and rest without a remedy.

'Oh yes, they asked me to say nothing; and to please them – so long as they were there – of course I promised. But what had happened to you?'

'I only went with you for the walk,' I said. 'I had then to come back to meet a friend.'

She showed her surprise. 'A friend – *you*?'

'Oh yes, I've a couple!' I laughed. 'But did the children give you a reason?'

'For not alluding to your leaving us? Yes; they said you'd like it better. *Do* you like it better?'

My face had made her rueful. 'No, I like it worse!' But after an instant I added: 'Did they say why I should like it better?'

'No; Master Miles only said "We must do nothing but what she likes!"'

'I wish indeed he would! And what did Flora say?'

'Miss Flora was too sweet. She said "Oh of course, of course!" – and I said the same.'

I thought a moment. 'You were too sweet too – I can hear you all. But none the less, between Miles and me, it's now all out.'

'All out?' My companion stared. 'But what, Miss?'

'Everything. It doesn't matter. I've made up my mind. I came home, my dear,' I went on, 'for a talk with Miss Jessel.'

I had by this time formed the habit of having Mrs. Grose literally well in hand in advance of my sounding that note; so that even now, as she bravely blinked under the signal of my word, I could keep her comparatively firm. 'A talk! Do you mean she spoke?'

'It came to that. I found her, on my return, in the schoolroom.'

'And what did she say?' I can hear the good woman still, and the candour of her stupefaction.

'That she suffers the torments—!'

It was this, of a truth, that made her, as she filled out my picture, gape. 'Do you mean,' she faltered '– of the lost?'

'Of the lost. Of the damned. And that's why, to share them—' I faltered myself with the horror of it.

But my companion, with less imagination, kept me up. 'To share them—?'

'She wants Flora.' Mrs. Grose might, as I gave it to her, fairly have fallen away from me had I not been prepared. I still held her there, to show I was. 'As I've told you, however, it doesn't matter.'

'Because you've made up your mind? But to what?'

'To everything.'

'And what do you call "everything"?'

'Why to sending for their uncle.'

'Oh Miss, in pity do,' my friend broke out.

'Ah but I will, I *will*! I see it's the only way. What's "out", as I told you, with Miles is that if he thinks I'm afraid to – and has ideas of what he gains by that – he shall see he's mistaken. Yes,

yes; his uncle shall have it here from me on the spot (and before the boy himself if necessary) that if I'm to be reproached with having done nothing again about more school—'

'Yes, Miss—' my companion pressed me.

'Well, there's that awful reason.'

There were now clearly so many of these for my poor colleague that she was excusable for being vague. 'But – a – which?'

'Why the letter from his old place.'

'You'll show it to the master?'

'I ought to have done so on the instant.'

'Oh no!' said Mrs. Grose with decision.

'I'll put it before him,' I went on inexorably, 'that I can't undertake to work the question on behalf of a child who has been expelled—'

'For we've never in the least known what!' Mrs. Grose declared.

'For wickedness. For what else – when he's so clever and beautiful and perfect? Is he stupid? Is he untidy? Is he infirm? Is he ill-natured? He's exquisite – so it can be only *that*; and that would open up the whole thing. After all,' I said, 'it's their uncle's fault. If he left here such people—!'

'He didn't really in the least know them. The fault's mine.' She had turned quite pale.

'Well, you shan't suffer,' I answered.

'The children shan't!' she emphatically returned.

I was silent a while; we looked at each other. 'Then what am I to tell him?'

'You needn't tell him anything. *I'll* tell him.'

I measured this. 'Do you mean you'll write—?' Remembering she couldn't, I caught myself up. 'How do you communicate?'

'I tell the bailiff. *He* writes.'

'And should you like him to write our story?'

My question had a sarcastic force that I had not fully intended, and it made her after a moment inconsequently break down. The tears were again in her eyes. 'Ah Miss, *you* write!'

'Well – to-night,' I at last returned; and on this we separated.

XVII

I went so far, in the evening, as to make a beginning. The weather had changed back, a great wind was abroad, and beneath the lamps, in my room, with Flora at peace beside me, I sat for a long time before a blank sheet of paper and listened to the last of the rain and the batter of the gusts. Finally I went out, taking a candle; I crossed the passage and listened a minute at Miles's door. What, under my endless obsession, I had been impelled to listen for was some betrayal of his not being at rest, and I presently caught one, but not in the form I had expected. His voice tinkled out. 'I say, you there – come in.' It was gaiety in the gloom!

I went in with my light and found him in bed, very wide awake but very much at his ease. 'Well, what are *you* up to?' he asked with a grace of sociability in which it occurred to me that Mrs. Grose, had she been present, might have looked in vain for proof that anything was 'out'.

I stood over him with my candle. 'How did you know I was there?'

'Why of course I heard you. Did you fancy you made no noise? You're like a troop of cavalry!' he beautifully laughed.

'Then you weren't asleep?'

'Not much! I lie awake and think.'

I had put my candle, designedly, a short way off, and then, as he held out his friendly old hand to me, had sat down on the edge of his bed. 'What is it,' I asked, 'that you think of?'

'What in the world, my dear, but *you*?'

'Ah the pride I take in your appreciation doesn't insist on that! I had so far rather you slept.'

'Well, I think also, you know, of this queer business of ours.'

I marked the coolness of his firm little hand. 'Of what queer business, Miles?'

'Why the way you bring me up. And all the rest!'

I fairly held my breath a minute, and even from my glimmering taper there was light enough to show how he smiled up at me from his pillow. 'What do you mean by all the rest?'

'Oh you know, you know!'

I could say nothing for a minute, though I felt as I held his hand and our eyes continued to meet that my silence had all the air of admitting his charge and that nothing in the whole world of reality was perhaps at that moment so fabulous as our actual relation. 'Certainly you shall go back to school,' I said, 'if it be that that troubles you. But not to the old place – we must find another, a better. How could I know it did trouble you, this question, when you never told me so, never spoke of it at all?' His clear listening face, framed in its smooth whiteness, made him for the minute as appealing as some wistful patient in a children's hospital; and I would have given, as the resemblance came to me, all I possessed on earth really to be the nurse or the sister of charity who might have helped to cure him. Well, even as it was I perhaps might help! 'Do you know you've never said a word to me about your school – I mean the old one; never mentioned it in any way?'

He seemed to wonder; he smiled with the same loveliness. But he clearly gained time; he waited, he called for guidance. 'Haven't I?' It wasn't for *me* to help him – it was for the thing I had met!

Something in his tone and the expression of his face, as I got this from him, set my heart aching with such a pang as it had never yet known; so unutterably touching was it to see his little brain puzzled and his little resources taxed to play, under the spell laid on him, a part of innocence and consistency. 'No, never – from the hour you came back. You've never mentioned to me one of your masters, one of your comrades, nor the least little thing that ever happened to you at school. Never, little Miles – no never – have you given me an inkling of anything that *may* have happened there. Therefore you can fancy how much I'm in the dark. Until you came out, that way, this morning, you had since the first hour I saw you scarce even made a reference to anything in your previous life. You seemed so perfectly to accept the present.' It was extraordinary how my absolute conviction of his secret precocity – or whatever I might call the poison of an influence that I dared but half-phrase – made him, in spite of the faint breath of his inward trouble, appear as accessible as an older person, forced me to treat him as an intelligent equal. 'I thought you wanted to go on as you are.'

It struck me that at this he just faintly coloured. He gave, at any rate, like a convalescent slightly fatigued, a languid shake of his head. 'I don't – I don't. I want to get away.'

'You're tired of Bly?'

'Oh no, I like Bly.'

'Well then—?'

'Oh *you* know what a boy wants!'

I felt I didn't know so well as Miles, and I took temporary refuge. 'You want to go to your uncle?'

Again, at this, with his sweet ironic face, he made a movement on the pillow. 'Ah you can't get off with that!'

I was silent a little, and it was I now, I think, who changed colour. 'My dear, I don't want to get off!'

'You can't even if you do. You can't, you can't!' – he lay beautifully staring. 'My uncle must come down and you must completely settle things.'

'If we do,' I returned with some spirit, 'you may be sure it will be to take you quite away.'

'Well, don't you understand that that's exactly what I'm working for? You'll have to *tell* him – about the way you've let it all drop: you'll have to tell him a tremendous lot!'

The exultation with which he uttered this helped me somehow for the instant to meet him rather more. 'And how much will *you*, Miles, have to tell him? There are things he'll ask you!'

He turned it over. 'Very likely. But what things?'

'The things you've never told me. To make up his mind what to do with you. He can't send you back—'

'I don't want to go back!' he broke in. 'I want a new field.'

He said it with admirable serenity, with positive unimpeachable gaiety; and doubtless it was that very note that most evoked for me the poignancy, the unnatural childish tragedy, of his probable reappearance at the end of three months with all this bravado and still more dishonour. It overwhelmed me now that I should never be able to bear that, and it made me let myself go. I threw myself upon him and in the tenderness of my pity I embraced him. 'Dear little Miles, dear little Miles—!'

My face was close to his, and he let me kiss him, simply taking it with indulgent good humour. 'Well, old lady?'

'Is there nothing – nothing at all that you want to tell me?'

He turned off a little, facing round toward the wall and holding up his hand to look at as one had seen sick children look. 'I've told you – I told you this morning.'

Oh I was sorry for him! 'That you just want me not to worry you?'

He looked round at me now as if in recognition of my understanding him; then ever so gently, 'To let me alone,' he replied.

There was even a strange little dignity in it, something that made me release him, yet, when I had slowly risen, linger beside him. God knows *I* never wished to harass him, but I felt that merely, at this, to turn my back on him was to abandon or, to put it more truly, lose him. 'I've just begun a letter to your uncle,' I said.

'Well then, finish it!'

I waited a minute. 'What happened before?'

He gazed up at me again. 'Before what?'

'Before you came back. And before you went away.'

For some time he was silent, but he continued to meet my eyes. 'What happened?'

It made me, the sound of the words, in which it seemed to me I caught for the very first time a small faint quaver of consenting consciousness – it made me drop on my knees beside the bed and seize once more the chance of possessing him. 'Dear little Miles, dear little Miles, if you *knew* how I want to help you! It's only that, it's nothing but that, and I'd rather die than give you a pain or do you a wrong – I'd rather die than hurt a hair of you. Dear little Miles' – oh I brought it out now even if I *should* go too far – 'I just want you to help me to save you!' But I knew in a moment after this that I had gone too far. The answer to my appeal was instantaneous, but it came in the form of an extraordinary blast and chill, a gust of frozen air and a shake of the room as great as if, in the wild wind, the casement had crashed in. The boy gave a loud high shriek which, lost in the rest of the shock of sound, might have seemed, indistinctly, though I was so close to him, a note either of jubilation or of terror. I jumped to my feet again and was conscious of darkness. So for a moment we remained, while I stared about me and saw the drawn curtains unstirred and the window still tight. 'Why the candle's out!' I then cried.

'It was I who blew it, dear!' said Miles.

XVIII

The next day, after lessons, Mrs. Grose found a moment to say to me quietly: 'Have you written, Miss?'

'Yes – I've written.' But I didn't add – for the hour – that my letter, sealed and directed, was still in my pocket. There would be time enough to send it before the messenger should go to the village. Meanwhile there had been on the part of my pupils no more brilliant, more exemplary morning. It was exactly as if they had both had at heart to gloss over any recent little friction. They performed the dizziest feats of arithmetic, soaring quite out of *my* feeble range, and perpetrated, in higher spirits than ever, geographical and historical jokes. It was conspicuous of course in Miles in particular that he appeared to wish to show how easily he could let me down. This child, to my memory, really lives in a setting of beauty and misery that no words can translate; there was a distinction all his own in every impulse he revealed; never was a small natural creature, to the uninformed eye all frankness and freedom, a more ingenious, a more extraordinary little gentleman. I had perpetually to guard against the wonder of contemplation into which my initiated view betrayed me; to check the irrelevant gaze and discouraged sigh in which I constantly both attacked and renounced the enigma of what such a little gentleman could have done that deserved a penalty. Say that, by the dark prodigy I knew, the imagination of all evil *had* been opened up to him: all the justice within me ached for the proof that it could ever have flowered into an act.

He had never at any rate been such a little gentleman as when, after our early dinner on this dreadful day, he came round to me and asked if I shouldn't like him for half an hour to play to me.

David playing to Saul[1] could never have shown a finer sense of the occasion. It was literally a charming exhibition of tact, of magnanimity, and quite tantamount to his saying outright: 'The true knights we love to read about never push an advantage too far. I know what you mean now: you mean that – to be let alone yourself and not followed up – you'll cease to worry and spy upon me, won't keep me so close to you, will let me go and come. Well, I "come", you see – but I don't go! There'll be plenty of time for that. I do really delight in your society and I only want to show you that I contended for a principle.' It may be imagined whether I resisted this appeal or failed to accompany him again, hand in hand, to the schoolroom. He sat down at the old piano and played as he had never played; and if there are those who think he had better have been kicking a football I can only say that I wholly agree with them. For at the end of a time that under his influence I had quite ceased to measure I started up with a strange sense of having literally slept at my post. It was after luncheon, and by the schoolroom fire, and yet I hadn't really in the least slept; I had only done something much worse – I had forgotten. Where all this time was Flora? When I put the question to Miles he played on a minute before answering, and then could only say: 'Why, my dear, how do *I* know?' – breaking moreover into a happy laugh which immediately after, as if it were a vocal accompaniment, he prolonged into incoherent extravagant song.

I went straight to my room, but his sister was not there; then, before going downstairs, I looked into several others. As she was nowhere about she would surely be with Mrs. Grose, whom in the comfort of that theory I accordingly proceeded in quest of. I found her where I had found her the evening before, but she met my quick challenge with blank scared ignorance. She had only supposed that, after the repast, I had carried off both the children; as to which she was quite in her right, for it was the very first time I had allowed the little girl out of my sight without some special provision. Of course now indeed she might be with the maids, so that the immediate thing was to look for her without an air of alarm. This we promptly arranged between us; but when, ten minutes later and in pursuance of our arrangement, we met in the hall, it was only to report on either side that after guarded enquiries we had altogether failed to trace her. For a minute there, apart from observation, we exchanged mute alarms, and I could feel with what high interest my friend returned me all those I had from the first given her.

'She'll be above,' she presently said – 'in one of the rooms you haven't searched.'

'No; she's at a distance.' I had made up my mind. 'She has gone out.'

Mrs. Grose stared. 'Without a hat?'

I naturally also looked volumes. 'Isn't that woman always without one?'

'She's with *her*?'

'She's with *her*!' I declared. 'We must find them.'

My hand was on my friend's arm, but she failed for the moment, confronted with such an account of the matter, to respond to my pressure. She communed, on the contrary, where she stood, with her uneasiness. 'And where's Master Miles?'

'Oh *he's* with Quint. They'll be in the schoolroom.'

'Lord, Miss!' My view, I was myself aware – and therefore I suppose my tone – had never yet reached so calm an assurance.

'The trick's played,' I went on; 'they've successfully worked their plan. He found the most divine little way to keep me quiet while she went off.'

'"Divine"?' Mrs. Grose bewilderedly echoed.

'Infernal then!' I almost cheerfully rejoined. 'He has provided for himself as well. But come!'

She had helplessly gloomed at the upper regions. 'You leave him—?'

'So long with Quint? Yes – I don't mind that now.'

She always ended at these moments by getting possession of my hand, and in this manner she could at present still stay me. But after gasping an instant at my sudden resignation, 'Because of your letter?' she eagerly brought out.

I quickly, by way of answer, felt for my letter, drew it forth, held it up, and then, freeing myself, went and laid it on the great hall-table. 'Luke will take it,' I said as I came back. I reached the house-door and opened it; I was already on the steps.

My companion still demurred: the storm of the night and the early morning had dropped, but the afternoon was damp and grey. I came down to the drive while she stood in the doorway. 'You go with nothing on?'

'What do I care when the child has nothing? I can't wait to dress,' I cried, 'and if you must do so I leave you. Try meanwhile yourself upstairs.'

'With *them*?' Oh on this the poor woman promptly joined me!

XIX

We went straight to the lake, as it was called at Bly, and I dare say rightly called, though it may have been a sheet of water less remarkable than my untravelled eyes supposed it. My acquaintance with sheets of water was small, and the pool of Bly, at all events on the few occasions of my consenting, under the protection of my pupils, to affront its surface in the old flat-bottomed boat moored there for our use, had impressed me both with its extent and its agitation. The usual place of embarkation was half a mile from the house, but I had an intimate conviction that, wherever Flora might be, she was not near home. She had not given me the slip for any small adventure, and, since the day of the very great one that I had shared with her by the pond, I had been aware, in our walks, of the quarter to which she most inclined. This was why I had now given to Mrs. Grose's steps so marked a direction – a direction making her, when she perceived it, oppose a resistance that showed me she was freshly mystified. 'You're going to the water, Miss? – you think she's *in*—?'

'She may be, though the depth is, I believe, nowhere very great. But what I judge most likely is that she's on the spot from which, the other day, we saw together what I told you.'

'When she pretended not to see—?'

'With that astounding self-possession! I've always been sure she wanted to go back alone. And now her brother has managed it for her.'

Mrs. Grosc still stood where she had stopped. 'You suppose they really *talk* of them?'

I could meet this with an assurance! 'They say things that, if we heard them, would simply appal us.'

'And if she *is* there—?'

'Yes?'

'Then Miss Jessel is?'

'Beyond a doubt. You shall see.'

'Oh thank you!' my friend cried, planted so firm that, taking it in, I went straight on without her. By the time I reached the pool, however, she was close behind me, and I knew that, whatever, to her apprehension, might befall me, the exposure of sticking to me struck her as her least danger. She exhaled a moan of relief as we at last came insight of the greater part of the water without a sight of the child. There was no trace of Flora on that nearer side of the bank where my observation of her had been most startling, and none on the opposite edge, where, save for a margin of some twenty yards, a thick copse came down to the pond. This expanse, oblong in shape, was so narrow compared to its length that, with its ends out of view, it might have been taken for a scant river. We looked at the empty stretch, and then I felt the suggestion in my friend's eyes. I knew what she meant and I replied with a negative headshake.

'No, no; wait! She has taken the boat.'

My companion stared at the vacant mooring-place and then again across the lake. 'Then where is it?'

'Our not seeing it is the strongest of proofs. She has used it to go over, and then has managed to hide it.'

'All alone – that child?'

'She's not alone, and at such times she's not a child: she's an old, old woman.' I scanned all the visible shore while Mrs. Grose took again, into the queer element I offered her, one of her plunges of submission; then I pointed out that the boat might perfectly be in a small refuge formed by one of the recesses of the pool, an indentation masked, for the hither side, by a projection of the bank and by a clump of trees growing close to the water.

'But if the boat's there, where on earth's *she*?' my colleague anxiously asked.

'That's exactly what we must learn.' And I started to walk further.

'By going all the way round?'

'Certainly, far as it is. It will take us but ten minutes, yet it's far enough to have made the child prefer not to walk. She went straight over.'

'Laws!' cried my friend again: the chain of my logic was ever too strong for her. It dragged her at my heels even now, and when we had got halfway round – a devious tiresome process, on ground much broken and by a path choked with overgrowth – I paused to give her breath. I sustained her with a grateful arm, assuring her that she might hugely help me; and this started us afresh, so that in the course of but few minutes more we reached a point from which we found the boat to be where I had supposed it. It had been intentionally left as much as possible out of sight and was tied to one of the stakes of a fence that came, just there, down to the brink and that had been an assistance to disembarking. I recognized, as I looked at the pair of short thick oars, quite safely drawn up, the prodigious character of the feat for a little girl; but I had by this time lived too long among wonders and had panted to too many livelier measures. There was a gate in the fence, through which we passed, and that brought us after a trifling interval more into the open. Then 'There she is!' we both exclaimed at once.

Flora, a short way off, stood before us on the grass and smiled as if her performance had now become complete. The next thing she did, however, was to stoop straight down and pluck – quite as if it were all she was there for – a big ugly spray of withered fern. I at once felt sure she had just come out of the copse. She waited for us, not herself taking a step, and I was conscious of the rare solemnity with which we presently approached her. She smiled and smiled, and we met; but it was all done in a silence by this time flagrantly ominous. Mrs. Grose was the first to break the spell: she threw herself on her knees and, drawing the child to her breast, clasped in a long embrace the little tender yielding body. While this dumb convulsion lasted I could only watch it – which I did the more intently when I saw Flora's face peep at me over our companion's shoulder. It was serious now – the flicker had left it; but it strengthened the pang with which I at that moment envied Mrs. Grose the simplicity of *her* relation. Still, all this while, nothing more passed between us save that

Flora had let her foolish fern again drop to the ground. What she and I had virtually said to each other was that pretexts were useless now. When Mrs. Grose finally got up she kept the child's hand, so that the two were still before me; and the singular reticence of our communion was even more marked in the frank look she addressed me. 'I'll be hanged,' it said, 'if *I'll* speak!'

It was Flora who, gazing all over me in candid wonder, was the first. She was struck with our bareheaded aspect. 'Why where are your things?'

'Where yours are, my dear!' I promptly returned.

She had already got back her gaiety and appeared to take this as an answer quite sufficient. 'And where's Miles?' she went on.

There was something in the small valour of it that quite finished me: these three words from her were in a flash like the glitter of a drawn blade the jostle of the cup that my hand for weeks and weeks had held high and full to the brim and that now, even before speaking, I felt overflow in a deluge. 'I'll tell you if you'll tell *me*—' I heard myself say, then heard the tremor in which it broke.

'Well, what?'

Mrs. Grose's suspense blazed at me, but it was too late now, and I brought the thing out handsomely. 'Where, my pet, is Miss Jessel?'

XX

Just as in the churchyard with Miles, the whole thing was upon us. Much as I had made of the fact that this name had never once, between us, been sounded, the quick smitten glare with which the child's face now received it fairly likened my breach of the silence to the smash of a pane of glass. It added to the interposing cry, as if to stay the blow, that Mrs. Grose at the same instant uttered over my violence – the shriek of a creature scared, or rather wounded, which, in turn, within a few seconds, was completed by a gasp of my own. I seized my colleague's arm. 'She's there, she's there!'

Miss Jessel stood before us on the opposite bank exactly as she had stood the other time, and I remember, strangely, as the first feeling now produced in me, my thrill of joy at having brought on a proof. She was there, so I was justified; she was there, so I was neither cruel nor mad. She was there for poor scared Mrs. Grose, but she was there most for Flora; and no moment of my monstrous time was perhaps so extraordinary as that in which I consciously threw out to her – with the sense that, pale and ravenous demon as she was, she would catch and understand it – an inarticulate message of gratitude. She rose erect on the spot my friend and I had lately quitted, and there wasn't in all the long reach of her desire an inch of her evil that fell short. This first vividness of vision and emotion were things of a few seconds, during which Mrs. Grose's dazed blink across to where I pointed struck me as showing that she too at last saw, just as it carried my own eyes precipitately to the child. The revelation then of the manner in which Flora was affected startled me in truth far more than it would have done to find her also merely agitated, for direct dismay was of course not what I had expected. Prepared and on her guard as our pursuit had actually made her, she would repress every betrayal; and I was therefore at once shaken by my first glimpse of the particular one for which I had not allowed. To see her, without a convulsion of her small pink face, not even feign to glance in the direction of the prodigy I announced, but only, instead of that, turn at *me* an expression of hard still gravity, an expression absolutely new and unprecedented and that appeared to read and accuse and judge me – this was a stroke that somehow converted the little girl herself into a figure portentous. I gaped at her coolness even though my certitude of her thoroughly seeing was never greater than at that instant, and then, in the immediate need to defend myself, I called her passionately to witness. 'She's there, you little unhappy thing – there, there, *there*, and you know it as well as you know me!' I had said shortly before to Mrs. Grose that she was not at these times a child, but an old, old woman, and my description of her couldn't have been more strikingly confirmed than in the way in which, for all notice of this, she simply showed me, without an expressional concession or admission, a countenance of deeper and deeper, of indeed suddenly quite fixed reprobation. I was by this time – if I can put the whole thing at all together – more appalled at what I may properly call her manner than at anything else, though it was quite simultaneously that I became aware of having Mrs. Grose also, and very formidably, to reckon with. My elder companion, the next moment, at any rate, blotted out everything but her own flushed face and her loud shocked protest, a burst of high disapproval. 'What a dreadful turn, to be sure, Miss! Where on earth do you see anything?'

I could only grasp her more quickly yet, for even while she spoke the hideous plain presence stood undimmed and undaunted. It had already lasted a minute, and it lasted while I continued, seizing my colleague, quite thrusting her at it and presenting her to it, to insist with my pointing hand. 'You don't see her exactly as *we* see? – you mean to say you don't now – *now*? She's as big as a blazing fire! Only look, dearest woman, *look*—!' She looked, just as I did, and gave me, with her deep groan of negation, repulsion, compassion – the mixture with her pity of her relief at her exemption – a sense, touching to me even then, that she would have backed me up if she had been able. I might well have needed that, for with this hard blow of the proof that her eyes were hopelessly sealed I felt my own situation horribly crumble, I felt – I *saw* – my livid predecessor press, from her position, on my defeat, and I took the measure, more than all, of what I should have from this instant to deal with in the astounding little attitude of Flora. Into this attitude Mrs. Grose immediately and violently entered, breaking, even while there pierced through my sense of ruin a prodigious private triumph, into breathless reassurance.

'She isn't there, little lady, and nobody's there – and you never see nothing, my sweet! How can poor Miss Jessel – when poor Miss Jessel's dead and buried? *We* know, don't we, love?' – and she appealed, blundering in, to the child. 'It's all a mere mistake and a worry and a joke – and we'll go home as fast as we can!'

Our companion, on this, had responded with a strange quick primness of propriety, and they were again, with Mrs. Grose on her feet, united, as it were, in shocked opposition to me. Flora continued to fix me with her small mask of disaffection, and even at that minute I prayed God to forgive me for seeming to see that, as she stood there holding tight to our friend's dress, her incomparable childish beauty had suddenly failed, had quite vanished. I've said it already – she was literally, she was hideously hard; she had turned common and almost ugly. 'I don't know what you mean. I see nobody. I see nothing. I never *have*. I think you're cruel. I don't like you!' Then, after this deliverance, which might have been that of a vulgarly pert little girl in the street, she hugged Mrs. Grose more closely and buried in her skirts the dreadful little face. In this position she launched an almost furious wail. 'Take me away, take me away – oh take me away from *her*!'

'From *me*?' I panted.

'From you – from you!' she cried.

Even Mrs. Grose looked across at me dismayed; while I had nothing to do but communicate again with the figure that, on the opposite bank, without a movement, as rigidly still as if catching, beyond the interval, our voices, was as vividly there for my disaster as it was not there for my service. The wretched child had spoken exactly as if she had got from some outside source each of her stabbing little words, and I could therefore, in the full despair of all I had to accept, but sadly shake my head at her. 'If I had ever doubted all my doubt would at present have gone. I've been living with the miserable truth, and now it has only too much closed round me. Of course I've lost you: I've interfered, and you've seen, under *her* dictation' – with which I faced, over the pool again, our infernal witness – 'the easy and perfect way to meet it. I've done my best, but I've lost you. Goodbye.' For Mrs. Grose I had an imperative, an almost frantic 'Go, go!' before which, in infinite distress, but mutely possessed of the little girl and clearly convinced, in spite of her blindness, that something awful had occurred and some collapse engulfed us, she retreated, by the way we had come, as fast as she could move.

Of what first happened when I was left alone I had no subsequent memory. I only knew that at the end of, I suppose, a quarter of an hour, an odorous dampness and roughness, chilling and piercing my trouble, had made me understand that I must have thrown myself, on my face, to the ground and given way to a wildness of grief. I must have lain there long and cried and wailed, for when I raised my head the day was almost done. I got up and looked a moment, through the twilight, at the grey pool and its blank haunted edge, and then I took, back to the house, my dreary and difficult course. When I reached the gate in the fence the boat, to my surprise, was gone, so that I had a fresh reflexion to make on Flora's extraordinary command of the situation. She passed that night, by the most tacit and, I should add, were not the word so grotesque a false note, the happiest of arrangements, with Mrs. Grose. I saw neither of them on my return, but on the other hand I saw, as by an ambiguous compensation, a great deal of Miles. I saw – I can use no other phrase – so much of him that it fairly measured more than it had ever measured. No evening I had passed at Bly was to have had the portentous quality of this one; in spite of which – and in spite also of the deeper depths of consternation that had opened beneath my feet – there was literally, in the ebbing actual, an extraordinarily sweet sadness. On reaching the house I had never so much as looked for the boy; I had simply gone straight to my room to change what I was wearing and to take in, at a glance, much material testimony to Flora's rupture. Her little belongings had all been removed. When later, by the school-room fire, I was served with tea by the usual maid, I indulged, on the article of my other pupil, in no enquiry whatever. He had his freedom now – he might have it to the end! Well, he did have it; and it consisted – in part at least – of his coming in at about eight o'clock and sitting down with me in silence. On the removal of the tea-things I had blown out the candles and drawn my chair closer: I was conscious of a mortal coldness and felt as if I should never again be warm. So when he appeared I was sitting in the glow with my thoughts. He paused a moment by the door as if to look at me; then – as if to share them – came to the other side of the hearth and sank into a chair. We sat there in absolute stillness; yet he wanted, I felt, to be with me.

XXI

Before a new day, in my room, had fully broken, my eyes opened to Mrs. Grose, who had come to my bedside with worse news. Flora was so markedly feverish that an illness was perhaps at hand; she had passed a night of extreme unrest, a night agitated above all by fears that had for their subject not in the least her former but wholly her present governess. It was not against the possible re-entrance of Miss Jessel on the scene that she protested – it was conspicuously and passionately against mine. I was at once on my feet, and with an immense deal to ask; the more that my friend had discernibly now girded her loins to meet me afresh. This I felt as soon as I had put to her the question of her sense of the child's sincerity as against my own. 'She persists in denying to you that she saw, or has ever seen, anything?'

My visitor's trouble truly was great. 'Ah Miss, it isn't a matter on which I can push her! Yet it isn't either, I must say, as if I much needed to. It has made her, every inch of her, quite old.'

'Oh I see her perfectly from here. She resents, for all the world like some high little personage, the imputation on her truthfulness and, as it were, her respectability. "Miss Jessel indeed – *she*!" Ah she's "respectable", the chit! The impression she gave me there yesterday was, I assure you, the very strangest of all: it was quite beyond any of the others. I *did* put my foot in it! She'll never speak to me again.'

Hideous and obscure as it all was, it held Mrs. Grose briefly silent; then she granted my point with a frankness which, I made sure, had more behind it. 'I think indeed, Miss, she never will. She do have a grand manner about it!'

'And that manner' – I summed it up – 'is practically what's the matter with her now.'

Oh that manner, I could see in my visitor's face, and not a little else besides! 'She asks me every three minutes if I think you're coming in.'

'I see – I see.' I too, on my side, had so much more than worked it out. 'Has she said to you since yesterday – except to repudiate her familiarity with anything so dreadful – a single other word about Miss Jessel?'

'Not one, Miss. And of course, you know,' my friend added, 'I took it from her by the lake that just then and there at least there *was* nobody.'

'Rather! And naturally you take it from her still.'

'I don't contradict her. What else can I do?'

'Nothing in the world! You've the cleverest little person to deal with. They've made them – their two friends, I mean – still cleverer even than nature did; for it was wondrous material to play on! Flora has now her grievance, and she'll work it to the end.'

'Yes, Miss; but to *what* end?'

'Why that of dealing with me to her uncle. She'll make me out to him the lowest creature—!'

I winced at the fair show of the scene in Mrs. Grose's face; she looked for a minute as if she sharply saw them together. 'And him who thinks so well of you!'

'He has an odd way – it comes over me now,' I laughed, '– of proving it! But that doesn't matter. What Flora wants of course is to get rid of me.'

My companion bravely concurred. 'Never again to so much as look at you.'

'So that what you've come to me now for,' I asked, 'is to speed me on my way?' Before she had time to reply, however, I had her in check. 'I've a better idea – the result of my reflexions. My going *would* seem the right thing, and on Sunday I was terribly near it. Yet that won't do. It's *you* who must go. You must take Flora.'

My visitor, at this, did speculate. 'But where in the world—?'

'Away from here. Away from *them*. Away, even most of all, now, from me. Straight to her uncle.'

'Only to tell on you—?'

'No, not "only"! To leave me, in addition, with my remedy.'

She was still vague. 'And what *is* your remedy?'

'Your loyalty, to begin with. And then Miles's.'

She looked at me hard. 'Do you think he—?'

'Won't, if he has the chance, turn on me? Yes, I venture still to think it. At all events I want to try. Get off with his sister as soon as possible and leave me with him alone.' I was amazed, myself, at the spirit I had still in reserve, and therefore perhaps a trifle the more disconcerted at the way in which, in spite of this fine example of it, she hesitated. 'There's one thing, of course,' I went on: 'they mustn't, before she goes, see each other for three seconds.' Then it came over me that, in spite of Flora's presumable sequestration from the instant of her return from the pool, it might already be too late. 'Do you mean,' I anxiously asked, 'that they *have* met?'

At this she quite flushed. 'Ah, Miss, I'm not such a fool as that! If I've been obliged to leave her three or four times, it has been each time with one of the maids, and at present, though she's alone, she's locked in safe. And yet – and yet!' There were too many things.

'And yet what?'

'Well, are you so sure of the little gentleman?'

'I'm not sure of anything but *you*. But I have, since last evening, a new hope. I think he wants to give me an opening. I do believe that – poor little exquisite wretch! – he wants to speak. Last evening, in the firelight and the silence, he sat with me for two hours as if it were just coming.'

Mrs. Grose looked hard through the window at the grey gathering day. 'And did it come?'

'No, though I waited and waited I confess it didn't, and it was without a breach of the silence, or so much as a faint allusion to his sister's condition and absence, that we at last kissed for good-night. All the same,' I continued, 'I can't, if her uncle sees her, consent to his seeing her brother without my having given the boy – and most of all because things have got so bad – a little more time.'

My friend appeared on this ground more reluctant than I

could quite understand. 'What do you mean by more time?'

'Well, a day or two – really to bring it out. He'll then be on *my* side – of which you see the importance. If nothing comes I shall only fail, and you at the worst have helped me by doing on your arrival in town whatever you may have found possible.' So I put it before her, but she continued for a little so lost in other reasons that I came again to her aid. 'Unless indeed,' I wound up, 'you really want *not* to go.'

I could see it, in her face, at last clear itself: she put out her hand to me as a pledge. 'I'll go – I'll go. I'll go this morning.'

I wanted to be very just. 'If you *should* wish still to wait I'd engage she shouldn't see me.'

'No, no: it's the place itself. She must leave it.' She held me a moment with heavy eyes, then brought out the rest. 'Your idea's the right one. I myself, Miss—'

'Well?'

'I can't stay.'

The look she gave me with it made me jump at possibilities. 'You mean that, since yesterday, you *have* seen—?'

She shook her head with dignity. 'I've *heard*!'

'Heard?'

'From that child – horrors! There!' she sighed with tragic relief. 'On my honour, Miss, she says things—!' But at this evocation she broke down; she dropped with a sudden cry upon my sofa and, as I had seen her do before, gave way to all the anguish of it.

It was quite in another manner that I for my part let myself go. 'Oh thank God!'

She sprang up again at this, drying her eyes with a groan. 'Thank God?'

'It so justifies me!'

'It does that, Miss!'

I couldn't have desired more emphasis, but I just waited. 'She's so horrible?'

I saw my colleague scarce knew how to put it. 'Really shocking.'

'And about me?'

'About you, Miss – since you must have it. It's beyond everything, for a young lady; and I can't think wherever she must have picked up—'

'The appalling language she applies to me? I can then!' I broke in with a laugh that was doubtless significant enough.

It only in truth left my friend still more grave. 'Well, perhaps I ought to also – since I've heard some of it before! Yet I can't bear it,' the poor woman went on while with the same movement she glanced, on my dressing-table, at the face of my watch. 'But I must go back.'

I kept her, however. 'Ah if you can't bear it—!'

'How can I stop with her, you mean? Why just *for* that: to get her away. Far from this,' she pursued, 'far from *them*—'

'She may be different? she may be free?' I seized her almost with joy. 'Then in spite of yesterday you *believe*—'

'In such doings?' Her simple description of them required, in the light of her expression, to be carried no further, and she gave me the whole thing as she had never done. 'I believe.'

Yes, it was a joy, and we were still shoulder to shoulder: if I might continue sure of that I should care but little what else happened. My support in the presence of disaster would be the same as it had been in my early need of confidence, and if my friend would answer for my honesty I would answer for all the rest. On the point of taking leave of her, none the less, I was to some extent embarrassed. 'There's one thing of course – it occurs to me – to remember. My letter giving the alarm will have reached town before you.'

I now felt still more how she had been beating about the bush and how weary at last it had made her. 'Your letter won't have got there. Your letter never went.'

'What then became of it?'

'Goodness knows! Master Miles—'

'Do you mean *he* took it?' I gasped.

She hung fire, but she overcame her reluctance. 'I mean that I saw yesterday, when I came back with Miss Flora, that it wasn't where you had put it. Later in the evening I had the chance to question Luke, and he declared that he had neither noticed nor touched it.' We could only exchange, on this, one of our deeper mutual soundings, and it was Mrs. Grose who first brought up the plumb with an almost elate 'You see!'

'Yes, I see that if Miles took it instead he probably will have read it and destroyed it.'

'And don't you see anything else?'

I faced her a moment with a sad smile. 'It strikes me that by this time your eyes are open even wider than mine.'

They proved to be so indeed, but she could still almost blush to show it. 'I make out now what he must have done at school.' And she gave, in her simple sharpness, an almost droll disillusioned nod. 'He stole!'

I turned it over – I tried to be more judicial. 'Well – perhaps.'

She looked as if she found me unexpectedly calm. 'He stole *letters*!'

She couldn't know my reasons for a calmness after all pretty shallow; so I showed them off as I might. 'I hope then it was to more purpose than in this case! The note, at all events, that I put on the table yesterday,' I pursued, 'will have given him so scant an advantage – for it contained only the bare demand for an interview – that he's already much ashamed of having gone so far for so little, and that what he had on his mind last evening was precisely the need of confession.' I seemed to myself for the instant to have mastered it, to see it all. 'Leave us, leave us' – I was already, at the door, hurrying her off. 'I'll get it out of him. He'll meet me. He'll confess. If he confesses he's saved. And if he's saved—'

'Then *you* are?' The dear woman kissed me on this, and I took her farewell. 'I'll save you without him!' she cried as she went.

XXII

Yet it was when she had got off – and I missed her on the spot – that the great pinch really came. If I had counted on what it would give me to find myself alone with Miles I quickly recognized that it would give me at least a measure. No hour of my stay in fact was so assailed with apprehensions as that of my coming down to learn that the carriage containing Mrs. Grose and my younger pupil had already rolled out of the gates. Now I *was*, I said to myself, face to face with the elements, and for much of the rest of the day, while I fought my weakness, I could consider that I had been supremely rash. It was a tighter place still than I had yet turned round in; all the more that, for the first time, I could see in the aspect of others a confused reflexion of the crisis. What had happened naturally caused them all to stare; there was too little of the explained, throw out whatever we might, in the suddenness of my colleague's act. The maids and the men looked blank; the effect of which on my nerves was an aggravation until I saw the necessity of making it a positive aid. It was in short by just clutching the helm that I avoided total wreck; and I dare say that, to bear up at all, I became that morning very grand and very dry. I welcomed the consciousness that I was charged with much to do, and I caused it to be known as well that, left thus to myself, I was quite remarkably firm. I wandered with that manner, for the next hour or two, all over the place and looked, I have no doubt, as if I were ready for any onset. So, for the benefit of whom it might concern, I paraded with a sick heart.

The person it appeared least to concern proved to be, till dinner, little Miles himself. My perambulations had given me meanwhile no glimpse of him, but they had tended to make more public the change taking place in our relation as a consequence of his having at the piano, the day before, kept me, in Flora's interest, so beguiled and befooled. The stamp of publicity had of course been fully given by her confinement and departure, and the change itself was now ushered in by our non-observance of the regular custom of the schoolroom. He had already disappeared when, on my way down, I pushed open his door, and I learnt below that he had breakfasted – in the presence of a couple of the maids – with Mrs. Grose and his sister. He had then gone out, as he said, for a stroll; than which nothing, I reflected, could better have expressed his frank view of the abrupt transformation of my office. What he would now permit this office to consist of was yet to be settled: there was at the least a queer relief – I mean for myself in especial – in the renouncement of one pretension. If so much had sprung to the surface I scarce put it too strongly in saying that what had perhaps sprung highest was the absurdity of our prolonging the fiction that I had anything more to teach him. It sufficiently stuck out that, by tacit little tricks in which even more than myself he carried out the care for my dignity, I had had to appeal to him to let me off straining to meet him on the ground of his true capacity. He had at any rate his freedom now; I was never to touch it again: as I had amply shown, moreover, when, on his joining me in the schoolroom the previous night, I uttered, in reference to the interval just concluded, neither challenge nor hint. I had too much, from this moment, my other ideas. Yet when he at last arrived the difficulty of applying them, the accumulations of my problem, were brought straight home to me by the beautiful little presence on which what had occurred had as yet, for the eye, dropped neither stain nor shadow.

To mark, for the house, the high state I cultivated I decreed that my meals with the boy should be served, as we called it, downstairs; so that I had been awaiting him in the ponderous pomp of the room outside the window of which I had had from Mrs. Grose, that first scared Sunday, my flash of something it would scarce have done to call light. Here at present I felt afresh – for I had felt it again and again – how my equilibrium depended on the success of my rigid will, the will to shut my eyes as tight as possible to the truth that what I had to deal with was, revoltingly, against nature. I could only get on at all by taking 'nature' into my confidence and my account, by treating my monstrous ordeal as a push in a direction unusual, of course, and unpleasant, but demanding after all, for a fair front, only another turn of the screw of ordinary human virtue. No attempt, none the less, could well require more tact than just this attempt to supply, one's self, *all* the nature. How could I put even a little of that article into a suppression of reference to what had occurred? How on the other hand could I make a reference without a new plunge into the hideous obscure? Well, a sort of answer, after a time, had come to me, and it was so far confirmed as that I was met, incontestably, by the quickened vision of what was rare in my little companion. It was indeed as if he had found even now – as he had so often found at lessons – still some other delicate way to ease me off. Wasn't there light in the fact which, as we shared our solitude, broke out with a specious glitter it had never yet quite worn? – the fact that (opportunity aiding, precious opportunity which had now come) it would be preposterous, with a child so endowed, to forego the help one might wrest from absolute intelligence? What had his intelligence been given him for but to save him? Mightn't one, to reach his mind, risk the stretch of a stiff arm across his character? It was as if, when we were face to face in the dining-room, he had literally shown me the way. The roast mutton was on the table and I had dispensed with attendance. Miles, before he sat down, stood a moment with his hands in his pockets and looked at the joint, on which he seemed on the point of passing some humorous judgement. But what he presently produced was: 'I say, my dear, is she really very awfully ill?'

'Little Flora? Not so bad but that she'll presently be better. London will set her up. Bly had ceased to agree with her. Come here and take your mutton.'

He alertly obeyed me, carried the plate carefully to his seat and, when he was established, went on. 'Did Bly disagree with her so terribly all at once?'

'Not so suddenly as you might think. One had seen it coming on.'

'Then why didn't you get her off before?'

'Before what?'

'Before she became too ill to travel.'

I found myself prompt. 'She's *not* too ill to travel; she only might have become so if she had stayed. This was just the moment to seize. The journey will dissipate the influence' – oh I was grand! – 'and carry it off.'

'I see, I see' – Miles, for that matter, was grand too. He settled to his repast with the charming little 'table manner' that, from the day of his arrival, had relieved me of all grossness of admonition. Whatever he had been expelled from school for, it wasn't for ugly feeding. He was irreproachable, as always, today; but was unmistakeably more conscious. He was discernibly trying to take for granted more things than he found, without assistance, quite easy; and he dropped into peaceful silence while he felt his situation. Our meal was of the briefest – mine a vain pretence, and I had the things immediately removed. While this was done Miles stood again with his hands in his little pockets and his back to me – stood and looked out of the wide window through which, that other day, I had seen what pulled me up. We continued silent while the maid was with us – as silent, it whimsically occurred to me, as some young couple who, on their wedding-journey, at the inn, feel shy in the presence of the waiter. He turned round only when the waiter had left us. 'Well – so we're alone!'

XXIII

'Oh more or less.' I imagine my smile was pale. 'Not absolutely. We shouldn't like that!' I went on.

'No – I suppose we shouldn't. Of course we've the others.'

'We've the others – we've indeed the others,' I concurred.

'Yet even though we have them,' he returned, still with his hands in his pockets and planted there in front of me, 'they don't much count, do they?'

I made the best of it, but I felt wan. 'It depends on what you call "much"!'

'Yes' – with all accommodation – 'everything depends!' On this, however, he faced to the window again and presently reached it with his vague restless cogitating step. He remained there a while with his forehead against the glass, in contemplation of the stupid shrubs I knew and the dull things of November. I had always my hypocrisy of 'work', behind which I now gained the sofa. Steadying myself with it there as I had repeatedly done at those moments of torment that I have described as the moments of my knowing the children to be given to something from which I was barred, I sufficiently obeyed my habit of being prepared for the worst. But an extraordinary impression dropped on me as I extracted a meaning from the boy's embarrassed back – none other than the impression that I was not barred now. This inference grew in a few minutes to sharp intensity and seemed bound up with the direct perception that it was positively *he* who was. The frames and squares of the great window were a kind of image, for him, of a kind of failure. I felt that I saw him, in any case, shut in or shut out. He was admirable but not comfortable: I took it in with a throb of hope. Wasn't he looking through the haunted pane for something he couldn't see? – and wasn't it the first time in the whole business that he had known such a lapse? The first, the very first: I found it a splendid portent. It made him anxious, though he watched himself; he had been anxious all day and, even while in his usual sweet little manner he sat at table, had needed all his small strange genius to give it a gloss. When he at last turned round to meet me it was almost as if this genius had succumbed. 'Well, I think I'm glad Bly agrees with *me*!'

'You'd certainly seem to have seen, these twenty-four hours, a good deal more of it than for some time before. I hope,' I went on bravely, 'that you've been enjoying yourself.'

'Oh yes, I've been ever so far; all round about – miles and miles away. I've never been so free.'

He had really a manner of his own, and I could only try to keep up with him. 'Well, do you like it?'

He stood there smiling; then at last he put into two words – 'Do *you*?' – more discrimination than I had ever heard two words contain. Before I had time to deal with that, however, he continued as if with the sense that this was an impertinence to be softened. 'Nothing could be more charming than the way you take it, for of course if we're alone together now it's you that are alone most. But I hope,' he threw in, 'you don't particularly mind!'

'Having to do with you?' I asked. 'My dear child, how can I help minding? Though I've renounced all claim to your company – you're so beyond me – I at least greatly enjoy it. What else should I stay on for?'

He looked at me more directly, and the expression of his face, graver now, struck me as the most beautiful I had ever found in it. 'You stay on just for *that*?'

'Certainly. I stay on as your friend and from the tremendous interest I take in you till something can be done for you that may be more worth your while. That needn't surprise you.' My voice trembled so that I felt it impossible to suppress the shake. 'Don't you remember how I told you, when I came and sat on your bed the night of the storm, that there was nothing in the world I wouldn't do for you?'

'Yes, yes!' He, on his side, more and more visibly nervous, had a tone to master; but he was so much more successful than I that, laughing out through his gravity, he could pretend we were pleasantly jesting. 'Only that, I think, was to get me to do something for *you*!'

'It was partly to get you to do something,' I conceded. 'But, you know, you didn't do it.'

'Oh yes,' he said with the brightest superficial eagerness, 'you wanted me to tell you something.'

'That's it. Out, straight out. What you have on your mind, you know.'

'Ah then is *that* what you've stayed over for?'

He spoke with a gaiety through which I could still catch the finest little quiver of resentful passion; but I can't begin to express the effect upon me of an implication of surrender even so faint. It was as if what I had yearned for had come at last only to astonish me. 'Well, yes – I may as well make a clean breast of it. It was precisely for that.'

He waited so long that I supposed it for the purpose of repudiating the assumption on which my action had been founded; but what he finally said was: 'Do you mean now – here?'

'There couldn't be a better place or time.' He looked round him uneasily, and I had the rare – oh the queer! – impression of the very first symptom I had seen in him of the approach of immediate fear. It was as if he were suddenly afraid of me – which struck me indeed as perhaps the best thing to make him. Yet in the very pang of the effort I felt it vain to try sternness, and I heard myself the next instant so gentle as to be almost grotesque. 'You want so to go out again?'

'Awfully!' He smiled at me heroically, and the touching little bravery of it was enhanced by his actually flushing with pain. He had picked up his hat, which he had brought in, and stood twirling it in a way that gave me, even as I was just nearly reaching port, a perverse horror of what I was doing. To do it in *any* way was an act of violence, for what did it consist of but the obtrusion of the idea of grossness and guilt on a small helpless creature who had been for me a revelation of the possibilities of beautiful intercourse? Wasn't it base to create for a being so exquisite a mere alien awkwardness? I suppose I now read into our situation a clearness it couldn't have had at the time, for I seem to see our poor eyes already lighted with some spark of a prevision of the anguish that was to come. So we circled about with terrors and scruples, fighters not daring to close. But it was for each other we feared! That kept us a little longer suspended and unbruised. 'I'll tell you everything,' Miles said – 'I mean I'll tell you anything you like. You'll stay on with me, and we shall both be all right, and I *will* tell you – I *will*. But not now.'

'Why not now?'

My insistence turned him from me and kept him once more at his window in a silence during which, between us, you might have heard a pin drop. Then he was before me again with the air of a person for whom, outside, some one who had frankly to be reckoned with was waiting. 'I have to see Luke.'

I had not yet reduced him to quite so vulgar a lie, and I felt proportionately ashamed. But, horrible as it was, his lies made up my truth. I achieved thoughtfully a few loops of my knitting. 'Well then go to Luke, and I'll wait for what you promise. Only in return for that satisfy, before you leave me, one very much smaller request.'

He looked as if he felt he had succeeded enough to be able still a little to bargain. 'Very much smaller—?'

'Yes, a mere fraction of the whole. Tell me' – oh my work preoccupied me, and I was off-hand! – 'if, yesterday afternoon, from the table in the hall, you took, you know, my letter.'

XXIV

My grasp of how he received this suffered for a minute from something that I can describe only as a fierce split of my attention – a stroke that at first, as I sprang straight up, reduced me to the mere blind movement of getting hold of him, drawing him close and, while I just fell for support against the nearest piece of furniture, instinctively keeping him with his back to the window. The appearance was full upon us that I had already had to deal with here: Peter Quint had come into view like a sentinel before a prison. The next thing I saw was that, from outside, he had reached the window, and then I knew that, close to the glass and glaring in through it, he offered once more to the room his white face of damnation. It represents but grossly what took place within me at the sight to say that on the second my decision was made; yet I believe that no woman so overwhelmed ever in so short a time recovered her command of the *act*. It came to me in the very horror of the immediate presence that the act would be, seeing and facing what I saw and faced, to keep the boy himself unaware. The inspiration – I can call it by no other name – was that I felt how voluntarily, how transcendently, I *might*. It was like fighting with a demon for a human soul, and when I had fairly so appraised it I saw how the human soul – held out, in the tremor of my hands, at arms' length – had a perfect dew of sweat on a lovely childish forehead. The face that was close to mine was as white as the face against the glass, and out of it presently came a sound, not low nor weak, but as if from much further away, that I drank like a waft of fragrance.

'Yes – I took it.'

At this, with a moan of joy, I enfolded, I drew him close; and while I held him to my breast, where I could feel in the sudden fever of his little body the tremendous pulse of his little heart, I kept my eyes on the thing at the window and saw it move and shift its posture. I have likened it to a sentinel, but its slow wheel, for a moment, was rather the prowl of a baffled beast. My present quickened courage, however, was such that, not too much to let it through, I had to shade, as it were, my flame. Meanwhile the glare of the face was again at the window, the scoundrel fixed as if to watch and wait. It was the very confidence that I might now defy him, as well as the positive certitude, by this time, of the child's unconsciousness, that made me go on. 'What did you take it for?'

'To see what you said about me.'

'You opened the letter?'

'I opened it.'

My eyes were now, as I held him off a little again, on Miles's own face, in which the collapse of mockery showed me how complete was the ravage of uneasiness. What was prodigious was that at last, by my success, his sense was sealed and his communication stopped: he knew that he was in presence, but knew not of what, and knew still less that I also was and that I did know. And what did this strain of trouble matter when my eyes went back to the window only to see that the air was clear again and – by my personal triumph – the influence quenched? There was nothing there. I felt that the cause was mine and that I should surely get *all*. 'And you found nothing!' – I let my elation out.

He gave the most mournful, thoughtful little headshake. 'Nothing.'

'Nothing, nothing!' I almost shouted in my joy.

'Nothing, nothing,' he sadly repeated.

I kissed his forehead; it was drenched. 'So what have you done with it?'

'I've burnt it.'

'Burnt it?' It was now or never. 'Is that what you did at school?'

Oh what this brought up! 'At school?'

'Did you take letters? – or other things?'

'Other things?' He appeared now to be thinking of something far off and that reached him only through the pressure of his anxiety. Yet it did reach him. 'Did I *steal*?'

I felt myself redden to the roots of my hair as well as wonder if it were more strange to put to a gentleman such a question or to see him take it with allowances that gave the very distance of his fall in the world. 'Was it for that you mightn't go back?'

The only thing he felt was rather a dreary little surprise. 'Did you know I mightn't go back?'

'I know everything.'

He gave me at this the longest and strangest look. 'Everything?'

'Everything. Therefore *did* you—?' But I couldn't say it again.

Miles could, very simply. 'No. I didn't steal.'

My face must have shown him I believed him utterly; yet my hands – but it was for pure tenderness – shook him as if to ask him why, if it was all for nothing, he had condemned me to months of torment. 'What then did you do?'

He looked in vague pain all round the top of the room and drew his breath, two or three times over, as if with difficulty. He might have been standing at the bottom of the sea and raising his eyes to some faint green twilight. 'Well – I said things.'

'Only that?'

'They thought it was enough!'

'To turn you out for?'

Never, truly, had a person 'turned out' shown so little to explain it as this little person! He appeared to weigh my question, but in a manner quite detached and almost helpless. 'Well, I suppose I oughtn't.'

'But to whom did you say them?'

He evidently tried to remember, but it dropped – he had lost it. 'I don't know?'

He almost smiled at me in the desolation of his surrender, which was indeed practically, by this time, so complete that I ought to have left it there. But I was infatuated – I was blind with victory, though even then the very effect that was to have brought him so much nearer was already that of added separation. 'Was it to every one?' I asked.

'No; it was only to—' But he gave a sick little headshake. 'I don't remember their names.'

'Were they then so many?'

'No – only a few. Those I liked.'

Those he liked? I seemed to float not into clearness, but into a darker obscure, and within a minute there had come to me out of my very pity the appalling alarm of his being perhaps innocent. It was for the instant confounding and bottomless, for if he *were* innocent what then on earth was I? Paralysed, while it lasted, by the mere brush of the question, I let him go a little, so that, with a deep-drawn sigh, he turned away from me again; which, as he faced toward the clear window, I suffered, feeling that I had nothing now there to keep him from. 'And did they repeat what you said?' I went on after a moment.

He was soon at some distance from me, still breathing hard and again with the air, though now without anger for it, of being confined against his will. Once more, as he had done before, he looked up at the dim day as if, of what had hitherto sustained him, nothing was left but an unspeakable anxiety. 'Oh yes,' he nevertheless replied – 'they must have repeated them. To those *they* liked,' he added.

There was somehow less of it than I had expected; but I turned it over. 'And these things came round—?'

'To the masters? Oh yes!' he answered very simply. 'But I didn't know they'd tell.'

'The masters? They didn't – they've never told. That's why I ask you.'

He turned to me again his little beautiful fevered face. 'Yes, it was too bad.'

'Too bad?'

'What I suppose I sometimes said. To write home.'

I can't name the exquisite pathos of the contradiction given to such a speech by such a speaker; I only know that the next instant I heard myself throw off with homely force: 'Stuff and nonsense!' But the next after that I must have sounded stern enough. 'What *were* these things?'

My sternness was all for his judge, his executioner; yet it made him avert himself again, and that movement made *me*, with a single bound and an irrepressible cry, spring straight upon him. For there again, against the glass, as if to blight his confession and stay his answer, was the hideous author of our woe – the white face of damnation. I felt a sick swim at the drop of my victory and all the return of my battle, so that the wildness of my veritable leap only served as a great betrayal. I saw him, from the midst of my act, meet it with a divination, and on the perception that even now he only guessed, and that the window was still to his own eyes free, I let the impulse flame up to convert the climax of his dismay into the very proof of his liberation. 'No more, no more, no more!' I shrieked to my visitant as I tried to press him against me.

'Is she *here*?' Miles panted as he caught with his sealed eyes the direction of my words. Then as his strange 'she' staggered me and, with a gasp, I echoed it, 'Miss Jessel, Miss Jessel!' he with sudden fury gave me back.

I seized, stupefied, his supposition – some sequel to what we had done to Flora, but this made me only want to show him that it was better still than that. 'It's not Miss Jessel! But it's at the window – straight before us. It's *there* – the coward horror, there for the last time!'

At this, after a second in which his head made the movement of a baffled dog's on a scent and then gave a frantic little shake for air and light, he was at me in a white rage, bewildered, glaring vainly over the place and missing wholly, though it now, to my sense, filled the room like the taste of poison, the wide overwhelming presence. 'It's *he*?'

I was so determined to have all my proof that I flashed into ice to challenge him. 'Whom do you mean by "he"?'

'Peter Quint – you devil!' His face gave again, round the room, its convulsed supplication. '*Where*?'

They are in my ears still, his supreme surrender of the name and his tribute to my devotion. 'What does he matter now, my own? – what will he *ever* matter? *I* have you,' I launched at the beast, 'but he has lost you for ever!' Then for the demonstration of my work,[1] 'There, *there*!' I said to Miles.

But he had already jerked straight round, stared, glared again, and seen but the quiet day. With the stroke of the loss I was so proud of he uttered the cry of a creature hurled over an abyss, and the grasp with which I recovered him might have been that of catching him in his fall. I caught him, yes, I held him – it may be imagined with what a passion; but at the end of a minute I began to feel what it truly was that I held. We were alone with the quiet day, and his little heart, dispossessed, had stopped.

From the Preface to the New York Edition

The following extract reprints the entire section on 'The Turn of the Screw' in Henry James's Preface to volume 12 of the New York Edition, containing 'The Aspern Papers', 'The Turn of the Screw', 'The Liar' and 'The Two Faces'.

This perfectly independent and irresponsible little fiction rejoices, beyond any rival on a like ground, in a conscious provision of prompt retort to the sharpest question that may be addressed to it. For it has the small strength if I shouldn't say rather the unattackable ease of a perfect homogeneity of being, to the very last grain of its virtue, all of a kind; the very kind, as happens, least apt to be baited by earnest criticism, the only sort of criticism of which account need be taken. To have handled again this so full-blown flower of high fancy is to be led back by it to easy and happy recognition. Let the first of these be that of the starting-point itself – the sense, all charming again, of the circle, one winter afternoon, round the hall-fire of a grave old country-house where (for all the world as if to resolve itself promptly and obligingly into convertible, into 'literary' stuff) the talk turned, on I forget what homely pretext, to apparitions and night-fears, to the marked and sad drop in the general supply, and still more in the general quality, of such commodities. The good, the really effective and heart-shaking ghost-stories (roughly so to term them) appeared all to have been told, and neither new crop nor new type in any quarter awaited us. The new type indeed, the mere modern 'psychical' case, washed clean of all queerness as by exposure to a flowing laboratory tap, and equipped with credentials vouching for this – the new type clearly promised little, for the more it was respectably certified the less it seemed of a nature to rouse the dear old sacred terror. Thus it was, I remember, that amid our lament for a beautiful lost form, our distinguished host expressed the wish that he might but have recovered for us one of the scantest of fragments of this form at its best. He had never forgotten the impression made on him as a young man by the withheld glimpse, as it were, of a dreadful matter that had been reported years before, and with as few particulars, to a lady with whom he had youthfully talked. The story would have been thrilling could she but have found herself in better possession of it, dealing as it did with a couple of small children in an out-of-the-way place, to whom the spirits of certain 'bad' servants, dead in the employ of the house, were believed to have appeared with the design of 'getting hold' of them. This was all, but there had been more, which my friend's old converser had lost the thread of: she could only assure him of the wonder of the allegations as she had anciently heard them made. He himself could give us but this shadow of a shadow – my own appreciation of which, I need scarcely say, was exactly wrapped up in that thinness. On the surface there wasn't much, but another grain, none the less, would have spoiled the precious pinch addressed to its end as neatly as some modicum extracted from an old silver snuff-box and held between finger and thumb. I was to remember the haunted children and the prowling servile spirits as a 'value', of the disquieting sort, in all conscience sufficient; so that when, after an interval, I was asked for something seasonable by the promoters of a periodical dealing in the time-honoured Christmas-tide toy, I bethought myself at once of the vividest little note for sinister romance that I had ever jotted down.

Such was the private source of 'The Turn of the Screw'; and I wondered, I confess, why so fine a germ, gleaming there in the wayside dust of life, had never been deftly picked up. The thing had for me the immense merit of allowing the imagination absolute freedom of hand, of inviting it to act on a perfectly clear field, with no 'outside' control involved, no pattern of the usual or the true or the terrible 'pleasant' (save always of course the high pleasantry of one's very form) to consort with. This makes in fact the charm of my second reference, that I find here a perfect example of an exercise of the imagination unassisted, unassociated – playing the game, making the score, in the phrase of our sporting day, off its own bat. To what degree the game was worth playing I needn't attempt to say: the exercise I have noted strikes me now, I confess, as the interesting thing, the imaginative faculty acting with the *whole* of the case on its hands. The exhibition involved is in other words a fairy-tale pure and simple – save indeed as to its springing not from an artless and measureless, but from a conscious and cultivated credulity. Yet the fairy-tale belongs mainly to either of two classes, the short and sharp and single, charged more or less with the compactness of anecdote (as to which let the familiars of our childhood, Cinderella and Blue-Beard and Hop o' my Thumb and Little Red Riding Hood and many of the gems of the Brothers Grimm directly testify), or else the long and loose, the copious, the various, the endless, where, dramatically speaking, roundness is quite sacrificed – sacrificed to fulness, sacrificed to exuberance, if one will: witness at hazard almost any one of the Arabian Nights. The charm of all these things for the distracted modern mind is in the clear field of experience, as I call it, over which we are thus led to roam; an annexed but independent world in which nothing is right save as we rightly imagine it. We have to do *that*, and we do it happily for the short spurt and in the smaller piece, achieving so perhaps beauty and lucidity; we flounder, we lose breath, on the other hand – that is we fail, not of continuity, but of an agreeable unity, of the 'roundness' in which beauty and lucidity largely reside – when we go in, as they say, for great lengths and breadths. And this, oddly enough, not because 'keeping it up' isn't abundantly within the compass of the imagination appealed to in certain conditions, but because the finer interest depends just on *how* it is kept up.

Nothing is so easy as improvisation, the running on and on of invention; it is sadly compromised, however, from the moment its stream breaks bounds and gets into flood. Then the waters may spread indeed, gathering houses and herds and crops and cities into their arms and wrenching off, for our amusement, the whole face of the land – only violating by the same stroke our sense of the course and the channel, which is our sense of the uses of a stream and the virtue of a story. Improvisation, as in the Arabian Nights, may keep on terms with encountered objects by sweeping them in and floating them on its breast; but the great effect it so loses – that of keeping on terms with itself. This is ever, I intimate, the hard thing for the fairy-tale; but by just so much as it struck me as hard did it in 'The Turn of the Screw' affect me as irresistibly prescribed. To improvise with extreme freedom and yet at the same time without the possibility of ravage, without the hint of a flood; to keep the stream, in a word, on something like ideal terms with itself: that was here my definite business. The thing was to aim at absolute singleness, clearness and roundness, and yet to depend on an imagination working freely, working (call it) with extravagance; by which law it wouldn't be thinkable except as free and wouldn't be amusing except as controlled. The merit of the tale, as it stands, is accordingly, I judge, that it has struggled successfully with its dangers. It is an excursion into chaos while remaining, like Blue-Beard and Cinderella, but an anecdote – though an anecdote amplified and highly emphasized and returning upon itself; as, for that matter, Cinderella and Blue-Beard return. I need scarcely add after this that it is a piece of ingenuity pure and simple, of cold artistic calculation, an *amusette*[1] to catch those not easily caught (the 'fun' of the capture of the merely witless being ever but small), the jaded, the disillusioned, the fastidious. Otherwise expressed, the study is of a conceived 'tone', the tone of suspected and felt trouble, of an inordinate and incalculable sort – the tone of tragic, yet of exquisite, mystification. To knead the subject of my young friend's, the supposititious narrator's, mystification thick, and yet strain the expression of it so clear and fine that beauty would result: no side of the matter so revives for me as that endeavour. Indeed if the artistic value of such an experiment be measured by the intellectual echoes it may again, long after, set in motion, the case would make in favour of this little firm fantasy – which I seem to see draw behind it to-day a train of associations. I ought doubtless to blush for thus confessing them so numerous that I can but pick among them for reference. I recall for instance a reproach made me by a reader capable evidently, for the time, of some attention, but not quite capable of enough, who complained that I hadn't sufficiently 'characterized' my young woman engaged in her labyrinth; hadn't endowed her with signs and marks, features and humours, hadn't in a word invited her to deal with her own mystery as well as with that of Peter Quint, Miss Jessel and the hapless children. I remember well, whatever the absurdity of its now coming back to me, my reply to that criticism – under which one's artistic, one's ironic heart shook for the instant almost to breaking. 'You indulge in that stricture at your ease, and I don't mind confiding to you that – strange as it may appear! – one has to choose ever so delicately among one's difficulties, attaching one's self to the greatest, bearing hard on those and intelligently neglecting the others. If one attempts to tackle them all one is certain to deal completely with none; whereas the effectual dealing with a few casts a blest golden haze under cover of which, like wanton mocking goddesses in clouds, the other find prudent to retire. It was "déjà très-joli",[2] in "The Turn of the Screw", please believe, the general proposition of our young woman's keeping crystalline her record of so many intense anomalies and obscurities – by which I don't of course mean her explanation of them, a different matter; and I saw no way, I feebly grant (fighting, at the best too, periodically, for every grudged inch of my space) to exhibit her in relations other than those; one of which, precisely, would have been her relation to her own nature. We have surely as much of her own nature as we can swallow in watching it reflect her anxieties and inductions. It constitutes no little of a character indeed, in such conditions, for a young person, as she says, "privately bred", that she is able to make her particular credible statement of such strange matters. She has "authority", which is a good deal to have given her, and I couldn't have arrived at so much had I clumsily tried for more.'

For which truth I claim part of the charm latent on occasion in the extracted reasons of beautiful things – putting for the beautiful always, in a work of art, the close, the curious, the deep. Let me place above all, however, under the protection of that presence the side by which this fiction appeals most to consideration: its choice of its way of meeting its gravest difficulty. There were difficulties not so grave: I had for instance simply to renounce all attempt to keep the kind and degree of impression I wished to produce on terms with the to-day so copious psychical record of cases of apparitions. Different signs and circumstances, in the reports, mark these cases; different things are done – though on the whole very little appears to be – by the persons appearing; the point is, however, that some things are never done at all: this negative quantity is large – certain reserves and proprieties and immobilities consistently impose themselves. Recorded and attested 'ghosts' are in other words as little expressive, as little dramatic, above all as little continuous and conscious and responsive, as is consistent with their taking the trouble – and an immense trouble they find it, we gather – to appear at all. Wonderful and interesting therefore at a given moment, they are inconceivable figures in an *action* – and 'The Turn of the Screw' was an action, desperately, or it was nothing. I had to decide in fine between having my apparitions correct and having my story 'good' – that is producing my impression of the dreadful, my designed horror. Good ghosts, speaking by book, make poor subjects, and it was clear that from the first my hovering prowling blighting presences, my pair of abnormal agents, would have to depart altogether from the rules. They would be agents in fact; there would be laid on them the dire duty of causing the situation to reek with the air of Evil. Their desire and their ability to do so, visibly measuring meanwhile their effect, together with their observed and described success – this was exactly my central idea; so that, briefly, I cast my lot with pure romance, the appearances conforming to the true type being so little romantic.

This is to say, I recognize again, that Peter Quint and Miss Jessel are not 'ghosts' at all, as we now know the ghost, but goblins, elves, imps, demons as loosely constructed as those of the old trials for witchcraft; if not, more pleasingly, fairies of the legendary order, wooing their victims forth to see them dance under the moon. Not indeed that I suggest their reducibility to any form of the pleasing pure and simple; they please at the best but through having helped me to express my subject all directly and intensely. Here it was – in the use made of them – that I felt a high degree of art really required; and here it is that, on reading the tale over, I find my precautions justified. The essence of the matter was the villainy of motive in the evoked predatory creatures; so that the result would be ignoble – by which I mean would be trivial – were this element of evil but feebly or inanely suggested. Thus arose on behalf of my idea the lively interest of a possible suggestion and process of *adumbration*; the question of how best to convey that sense of the depths of the sinister without which my fable would so woefully limp. Portentous evil – how was I to save that, as an intention on the part of my demon-spirits, from the drop, the comparative vulgarity, inevitably attending, throughout the whole range of possible brief illustration, the offered example, the imputed vice, the cited act, the limited deplorable presentable instance? To bring the bad dead back to life for a second round of badness is to warrant them as indeed prodigious, and to become hence as shy of specifications as of a waiting anti-climax. One had seen, in fiction, some grand form of wrong-doing, or better still of wrong-being, imputed, seen it promised and announced as by the hot breath of the Pit – and then, all lamentably, shrink to the compass of some particular brutality, some particular immorality, some particular infamy portrayed: with the result, alas, of the demonstration's falling sadly short. If *my* bad things, for 'The Turn of the Screw', I felt, should succumb to this danger, if they shouldn't seem sufficiently bad, there would be nothing for me but to hang my artistic head lower than I had ever known occasion to do.

The view of that discomfort and the fear of that dishonour, it accordingly must have been, that struck the proper light for my right, though by no means easy, short cut. What, in the last analysis, had I to give the sense of? Of their being, the haunting pair, capable, as the phrase is, of everything – that is of exerting, in respect to the children, the very worst action small victims so conditioned might be conceived as subject to. What would *be* then, on reflexion, this utmost conceivability? – a question to which the answer all admirably came. There is for such a case no eligible *absolute* of the wrong; it remains relative to fifty other elements, a matter of appreciation, speculation, imagination – these things moreover quite exactly in the light of the spectator's, the critic's, the reader's experience. Only make the reader's general vision of evil intense enough, I said to myself – and that already is a charming job – and his own experience, his own imagination, his own sympathy (with the children) and horror (of their false friends) will supply him quite sufficiently with all the particulars. Make him *think* the evil, make him think it for himself, and you are released from weak specifications. This ingenuity I took pains – as indeed great pains were required – to apply; and with a success apparently beyond my liveliest hope. Droll enough at the same time, I must add, some of the evidence – even when most convincing – of this success. How can I feel my calculation to have failed, my wrought suggestion not to have worked, that is, on my being assailed, as has befallen me, with the charge of a monstrous emphasis, the charge of all indecently expatiating? There is not only from beginning to end of the matter not an inch of expatiation, but my values are positively all blanks save so far as an excited horror, a promoted pity, a created expertness – on which punctual effects of strong causes no writer can ever fail to plume himself – proceed to read into them more or less fantastic figures. Of high interest to the author meanwhile – and by the same stroke a theme for the moralist – the artless resentful reaction of the entertained person who has abounded in the sense of the situation. He visits his abundance, morally, on the artist – who has but clung to an ideal of faultlessness. Such indeed, for this latter, are some of the observations by which the prolonged strain of that clinging may be enlivened!

Notes

1 *Raison de plus*: All the more reason (French).
2 *Harley Street*: A street in the City of Westminster, London, known for its prosperous residences and professional consulting rooms.

I

1 *fly*: One-horse carriage.
2 *one of Raphael's holy infants*: Raffaello Sanzio da Urbino (1483–1520), one of the greatest painters of the Renaissance; see, for example, his infant John the Baptist in *The Holy Family of Francis I* (1518), and the children in his *Canigiani Madonna* (1507).

IV

1 *a mystery of Udolpho or an insane, an unmentionable relative kept in unsuspected confinement*: The terrors of Anne Radcliffe's *Mysteries of Udolpho* (1794) are the offspring of fantasy feeding on coincidence; Mr Rochester keeps his mad wife hidden in the attic in Charlotte Brontë's *Jane Eyre* (1847).
2 *I should have found the trace, should have felt the wound and the dishonour*: In all versions of the text before the New York Edition, the sentence ends with 'trace'.

VI

1 *Sea of Azof*: A small and shallow sea in western Russia directly north of, and linked to, the Black Sea.

IX

1 *I find that I really hang back; but I must take my horrid plunge . . . push my dreadful way through it to the end*: The adjectives 'horrid' and 'dreadful' in this passage appear only in the New York Edition.

2 *Fielding's 'Amelia'*: Henry Fielding's *Amelia* (1751) is a melodrama of feminine intelligence fronting adversity and being rewarded by marriage and love.

X

1 *Mrs. Marcet*: Jane Marcet (1769–1858), author of popular elementary books on the natural sciences and political economy.

XII

1 *By writing to him that his house is poisoned and his little nephew and niece mad?*: In the periodical version, this sentence reads: 'By writing to him that I have the honour to inform him that they see the dead come back?'

XIII

1 *Goody Gosling's celebrated mot*: Possibly a displaced memory of the nursery rhyme (with application to Quint and Miss Jessel): 'Goosey goosey gander, whither shall I wander, / Upstairs, downstairs and in my lady's chamber; / There I met an old man who wouldn't say his prayers, / So I took him by the left leg, and threw him down the stairs.' *Mot* abbreviates the French *bon mot*, meaning a witty remark: here rather dryly intended.
2 *If it was a question of a scare . . . and it was essentially in the scared state that I drew my actual conclusions*: In all versions before the New York Edition, the end of this sentence reads: 'and it was in the condition of nerves produced by it that I made my actual inductions'.

XVIII

1 *David playing to Saul*: A reference to I Samuel 16.14–23; David plays the harp for Saul, and makes the evil spirit from the Lord depart.

XXIV

1 *the demonstration of my work*: The periodical version of the text reads: 'the demonstration of my triumph'.

FROM THE PREFACE TO THE NEW YORK EDITION

1 *amusette*: Trifle (French).
2 *déjà très-joli*: Nicely settled (French).